DECEPTIONS

"It's been a really great evening, Nicholas," Elizabeth said.

"For me, too," Nicholas agreed. He reached across the table to take Elizabeth's hand.

She smiled at him over her coffee. Then she caught sight of someone coming toward her across the restaurant. *He looks just like Todd!* Elizabeth thought.

Elizabeth blinked and looked again. It was Todd!

But Todd was in Sweet Valley with his parents, celebrating his mother's birthday.

Wasn't he?

No, Elizabeth realized. Todd Wilkins was right there, in that very room. And he was fast approaching her table.

Elizabeth had a terrible feeling in the pit of her stomach. Her brain reeled. What had gone wrong?

Bantam Books in the Sweet Valley High Series
Ask your bookseller for the books you have missed

SWEET VALLEY HIGH

DECEPTIONS

Written by
Kate William

Created by
FRANCINE PASCAL

BANTAM BOOKS
TORONTO • NEW YORK • LONDON • SYDNEY • AUCKLAND

RL5, IL age 12 and up

DECEPTIONS

A Bantam Book / December 1984
7 printings through January 1987

Sweet Valley High is a trademark of Francine Pascal

Conceived by Francine Pascal

Produced by Cloverdale Press, Inc.

Cover art by James Mathewuse

ISBN 0-553-26763-9

Published simultaneously in the United States and Canada

Bantam Books are published by Bantam Books, Inc. Its trademark, consisting of
the words "Bantam Books" and the portrayal of a rooster, is Registered in
U.S. Patent and Trademark Office and in other countries. Marca Registrada.
Bantam Books, Inc., 666 Fifth Avenue, New York, New York 10103.

DECEPTIONS

One

"Come on in," Elizabeth Wakefield said to the tall, good-looking boy who was standing in the doorway of the Wakefield home. But Nicholas Morrow didn't move. His dark, soulful eyes were riveted on Elizabeth. She gave him a ravishing smile and nodded in the direction of the living room. "Follow me. I'll tell my sister you're here." She turned and started toward the living room, where the party her twin was giving in her honor had already begun.

"No. Wait!" There was an urgency in Nicholas's tone that stopped Elizabeth in her tracks.

She turned slowly to face him and saw that he was staring at her as if mesmerized. It was the last thing on earth she expected from Nicholas Morrow.

She'd expected him to be handsome. And as Elizabeth glanced at Nicholas, she could see that his finely chiseled features looked as if they belonged on the cover of a magazine. His face would have put a Greek god to shame.

She'd also expected him to be intelligent. And she could tell that was true just by looking into his eyes.

She could tell he was compassionate, too. But someone who would be struck dumb at the sight of a girl? That was one thing Elizabeth had not heard about Nicholas Morrow.

What she had heard came mainly from her twin, Jessica, who practically went into a trance every time she mentioned Nicholas's name. That was not unusual for Jessica when a new and handsome boy appeared on the scene, but this time she'd gone overboard. Elizabeth had hardly been home an hour after her release from the kidnapper who'd held her captive before Jessica brought up the subject.

"Oh, Liz!" she'd said, with a sigh that only she could manage. "I've met the most gorgeous boy."

"Who is it this time?"

"Nicholas Morrow, that's who!"

"Nicholas Morrow. OK, tell me more."

"Well, he's rich!"

"And he drives a Porsche, like Bruce Patman, right?" Elizabeth asked.

"Wrong! Oh, Liz, he's so fabulously rich he can afford to zip around in a Jeep." Elizabeth raised an eyebrow, and Jessica quickly added, "Of course his father drives a Ferrari."

"Well, that makes everything all right," Elizabeth muttered.

Jessica assumed an injured look. "For your information, Liz," she said, "even people as rich as the Morrows have their troubles. Like Nicholas's sister, Regina." Jessica shook her head sadly. "She's deaf," she said in a low, sorrowful voice.

"Deaf? How awful!"

"Yes, she's been that way all her life. But except for a funny lilt in her speech and the tiniest slur, she's just like everyone else."

"But if she can't hear . . ." Elizabeth began.

"She reads lips," Jessica explained. She was quiet for a few seconds, then she suddenly burst out with, "Liz, you should see the Morrow house. It's like a castle. You'd think the Queen of England lived there."

"Or Prince Charming?" Elizabeth asked, laughing.

A dreamy, faraway look crept into Jessica's eyes. "Or Prince Charming," she whispered.

Yes, Prince Charming, Elizabeth thought as she looked at Nicholas now. No wonder Jessica had likened this handsome boy to a fairy-tale prince. And it was no wonder that Nicholas had confused Elizabeth, at first, with Jessica. The twins were identical down to the dimples in their left cheeks.

Both girls were spectacular, with the all-American good looks that made them the envy of every other girl in Sweet Valley. They were a

3

perfectly proportioned five-foot-six, with silken, sun-streaked hair that fell to their shoulders. Their sparkling blue-green eyes were the color of the Pacific Ocean. The only difference between the two was the tiny mole on Elizabeth's right shoulder.

But beyond their appearance, Jessica and Elizabeth were as different as night and day. While Jessica prided herself on being clever and devious, Elizabeth was fairness and honesty personified.

Now, as Elizabeth looked at Nicholas, she noticed the hesitation in his eyes. In an effort to put him at ease, Elizabeth held her hands out to him. "Come on in," she said. "The party's just beginning."

Elizabeth led Nicholas into the living room, where The Droids, Sweet Valley High's own rock band, were belting out a fast, frantic number.

Todd Wilkins, Elizabeth's steady boyfriend, stood by the makeshift bandstand, tapping his foot to the music. When he saw Elizabeth his face lit up with a broad smile, and he started toward her.

At the same time Jessica, who was talking to Cara Walker, her best friend, caught sight of Nicholas Morrow. Breaking off her conversation in midsentence, she started across the room toward him. Just then, the doorbell rang.

"Jess, can you get it this time?" Elizabeth asked.

"I was just on my way," Jessica lied. She gave Nicholas a dazzling smile.

"Hi, Jessica," Nicholas said absent-mindedly.

At that moment The Droids switched from heavy rock to a dreamy, romantic song. Nicholas turned to Elizabeth. "Want to dance?" Nicholas asked.

Elizabeth had hoped to dance with Todd. But as hostess, she thought she should try to make Nicholas feel welcome. "Sure," she replied, smiling at Todd. She led Nicholas over to where her best friend Enid and Enid's boy-friend George Warren were dancing.

Nicholas put an arm around her, and they began to glide across the floor gracefully. Nicholas smiled down at Elizabeth. "Hey!" he said suddenly. "This song is about you!"

Elizabeth listened intently to the words Dana Larson, The Droids' lead singer, caressed in a soft, sexy voice. "Oh, Nicholas!" she said. "You're right. She must have written it to welcome me back." Her eyes misted over. "Aren't the kids at Sweet Valley just the greatest?"

"You can say that again."

"Think you'll like it here?" Elizabeth asked.

"I already do," Nicholas said, gazing into her eyes. But when he said, "You're very pretty, Elizabeth," she decided it was time to direct the conversation away from herself and toward him.

5

"My spies tell me," she murmured, "that you're going to college next year."

"Your spies are right," he said. "What else?"

"That you're taking this year off to learn your father's business."

"Right again! And did they tell you what that business is?"

"Computers," Elizabeth said.

"Very clever, those spies of yours. Any more information to report?"

"Not much," Elizabeth said. She cocked her head to one side, as if trying to remember. "On the other hand, my crystal ball . . ."

"Ah-ha! The crystal ball! What does that say?"

"First," she said, laughing, "that the music's stopped."

"Then?" Nicholas prompted.

"That I haven't said hello to Robin Wilson and Allen Walters, and I should do it now." With that as an excuse, Elizabeth headed for the buffet table set up in the kitchen, where Robin and Allen had just gone.

Allen had just poured a Diet Coke for Robin and was heaping his own plate with sandwiches when Elizabeth came up and threw her arms around Robin.

"Liz!" Robin cried out, hugging her. "It's so wonderful that you're home again."

Elizabeth placed a finger on her friend's lips. "Let's not talk about the kidnapping anymore," she said. Now that the ordeal was behind her she wanted to forget about it.

Robin changed the subject. "Isn't it great," she said enthusiastically, "that Max Dellon passed English and his family's letting him play with The Droids again. Oh, Liz"—she gave Elizabeth a thumbs up sign—"everything's OK now. Just like before."

"He's about the best guitar player I've ever heard," Nicholas said, breaking into the conversation.

"Nicholas!" Elizabeth exclaimed, spinning around in surprise. "I thought . . ."

"Not that I'd let you out of my sight?" he asked, laughing and shaking his head.

Elizabeth laughed too, but she felt uncomfortable. Stammering slightly she asked, "Robin, have you met Nicholas Morrow?"

Robin nodded. "Last week," she said. "At the party the night you—" She was about to say "disappeared," but she stopped just in time. "What I mean is . . ."

It was an awkward moment, but Nicholas glossed over it by holding out a hand to Elizabeth. "Hey," he said, "let's dance." Before she could say a word, he whirled her off.

As they danced, Elizabeth noticed her twin watching them from the other side of the room and trying to make eye contact with Nicholas. But he was so absorbed with Elizabeth that he didn't notice Jessica.

Elizabeth's own mind was on Todd, and her

eyes scanned the room until they lit on him. She gave him a warm smile, an unspoken promise that she'd join him as soon as the dance was over.

Nicholas, though, had other ideas. When the music ended, he said, "Come on. I want you to meet Regina. I just saw her come in with a group of kids from your school."

"I'd love to meet her," Elizabeth said truthfully, "but I have to—"

"I'd like you to meet her, too," Nicholas interrupted. "And I know she'd love to meet you. Besides, I want to see if she's OK. As an older brother I worry about her from time to time. Doesn't your brother worry about you?"

Elizabeth smiled. Eighteen-year-old Steven, like everyone else in the family, was more likely to worry about Jessica. But these days Steven was so preoccupied with his girlfriend, Tricia Martin, who had leukemia, that he rarely thought about anything else.

Instinctively Elizabeth looked around the room for him but didn't see him. That figured. As gloomy as Steven had been lately, he was probably in his bedroom now, avoiding human contact.

But she forgot about Steven as Nicholas led her through the downstairs rooms of the Wakefield house in search of his sister. He spotted her out on the patio, surrounded by Cara Walker, Lila Fowler, and a couple of other girls. Nicholas beamed with pride at the sight of his sister. "Regina's so friendly she attracts all kinds of people," he boasted.

And so rich, Elizabeth thought, *that she attracts snobs like Lila and Cara*.

As Nicholas and Elizabeth approached, Regina turned to greet them as if she'd known instinctively that Nicholas was there. Now Elizabeth saw how pretty Regina was. About the same age as the twins, she was tall and statuesque, as perfectly proportioned in her way as Jessica and Elizabeth were in theirs. She wore a stunning blue dress that highlighted her eyes and set off her light complexion. Her hair, worn long, was as dark and wavy as Nicholas's.

"Oh, Nicholas!" Elizabeth gasped. "She's so pretty."

Nicholas grinned. "You know, Elizabeth, I was really worried about how the move to Sweet Valley would affect Regina. But look at her now! She's going to fit right in with all the others."

"Oh, I'm sure she will," Elizabeth said. But if Regina was anything like her brother, who didn't seem to have the least desire to flaunt his wealth, those "others" weren't likely to include Cara Walker and Lila Fowler.

Nicholas spoke directly to his sister. She watched his face closely, reading his lips. "Regina, I want you to meet Elizabeth Wakefield," he said.

Elizabeth held out her hand. "Hi," she said pleasantly. "I'm really glad to meet you. I've heard a lot about you."

"Most of it from my brother, I'll bet," Regina said, giving him a quick glance and a brilliant smile. "Sometimes I wonder if I'm all he thinks about." She turned back to Elizabeth. "I've heard lots about you, too, Liz," Regina said. "And I'm dying to hear more." She was so sincere that Elizabeth didn't hesitate to answer her questions.

A few were about the school newspaper, *The Oracle*. "Are you really one of the reporters?" Regina asked.

"Yes, I am."

"And do you *really* write 'Eyes and Ears'?" Regina was referring to the light, humorous gossip column Elizabeth wrote each issue. Although her name never appeared above it, almost everyone knew that Elizabeth was the author.

"Yes, I write the column," Elizabeth said.

Regina clapped her hands together. "That's great, Liz. I've read it, and I think it's really good." She gave Elizabeth a warm, bright smile. "You must be about the most talented person in the whole valley," she added.

Elizabeth blushed, while Cara and Lila giggled. When Nicholas said, "You must be about the most modest, too," the red in Elizabeth's face deepened.

Still, a happy glow spread through her. She was on top of the world. Even the bored look on Lila Fowler's face and the slightly envious one on Cara Walker's didn't bother her, but she was glad when her sister's friends drifted back to the living room.

Watching them disappear, Elizabeth decided it was time to get back to the party. "Come on," she said. "Everyone will wonder where we are."

She linked arms with Regina and Nicholas and led them back into the house.

Two

The party was in full swing when the doorbell pealed again. "I'll get it," Elizabeth sang out. She dashed past Todd, who said, "That must be Ken Matthews. He told me he was coming late."

She gave him a quick, affectionate smile. "Ken Matthews?" she joked. "The name rings a bell." With Nicholas still at her heels, she sped to the door to greet the blond-haired captain of the Sweet Valley High football team.

Elizabeth went back to the living room, followed by Nicholas and Ken. She smiled at both of them, then looked around for Todd. Her gaze fell on Jessica instead. She was talking to Lila Fowler, but was scanning the room intently.

The moment Jessica caught sight of Elizabeth with Nicholas at her elbow, her smile faded, and her eyes narrowed dangerously. Without waiting for Lila to finish her sentence, she strode purposefully toward her twin and Nicholas.

Catching up with them, Jessica ignored

Elizabeth completely. But she gave Nicholas a dazzling smile. "Nicholas Morrow!" she said, scolding him gently. "Honestly, I've been looking absolutely everywhere for you. You know," she added, tilting her head coyly, "there must be a hundred and thirty-seven people waiting to meet you."

"Me?" Nicholas asked. "I thought I'd met everyone in town by now."

Jessica shook her head vigorously. "You haven't met my mother and father yet," she said, taking his arm. "Or my brother, Steven. Or dozens of people. And they're all dying to meet the famous Nicholas Morrow." With that, Jessica dragged him off, turning back once to shoot a triumphant glance in Elizabeth's direction.

Her parents were in her father's den, and Jessica quickly made the introductions. Nicholas shook hands with dark-haired, athletic-looking Ned Wakefield, and then with the twins' mother, Alice Wakefield. It was clear that Jessica and Elizabeth got their sun-kissed good looks from her. Like them, she was tanned and slender, with the same spun-silk blond hair. Youthful and very attractive, Alice Wakefield could easily have been mistaken for the twins' sister instead of their mother.

Nicholas spoke to the Wakefields politely, but his mind was still on Elizabeth. When Jessica led him off in search of Steven, he followed her reluctantly.

They found Steven at last, sitting on his bed

13

and looking glum. Jessica was glad he was alone. If Tricia Martin had been with him, she would have been obliged to introduce Nicholas to *her*, too.

Jessica had nothing against Tricia herself. But her father had a reputation as the town drunkard, and practically everyone knew that her sister, Betsy, was on drugs and frequently in trouble with the law. Jessica was ashamed to think that her brother was in love with a girl from that kind of family.

That night, though, Jessica had been spared the embarrassment she always felt in Tricia's presence. She introduced Nicholas to Steven, and the three of them made polite conversation for a few minutes before Jessica led Nicholas back down to the living room.

Jessica was glad she was wearing her sexiest outfit, a slinky black pantsuit with a plunging neckline. Preening a little, she smiled, then lowered her eyes. "It's so wonderful you're here in Sweet Valley, Nicholas," she said. "Honestly, this place was getting to be such a bore!"

"And that will change now that I'm here?" Nicholas asked.

Jessica looked at him. His eyes were cool, his gaze steady. But his lips twitched in a faint smile. Jessica heaved a great sigh. She could tell Nicholas was interested in her. "Oh, yes," she said. "Things will definitely change now that you're here!" She gave him a bewitching smile.

Nicholas averted his gaze and searched the

crowd for Elizabeth. At last he saw her chatting with her best friend, brown-haired, emerald-eyed Enid Rollins.

When Jessica noticed she'd lost his attention, she snapped her fingers in front of Nicholas's face. "Hey, where are you?" she asked.

Nicholas looked down into Jessica's eyes. "I'm in the clutches of one of the most beautiful girls in the world," he said.

A rush of excitement swept over Jessica. "How about dancing with her then?" she asked. "The music is terrific, and you must be about the world's greatest dancer. At least from what I've seen." Jessica took one of Nicholas's hands. "So what are we waiting for?"

"Not a thing," Nicholas said, falling into step with Jessica. She rested her head on his shoulder, looking up from time to time into his eyes. Nicholas smiled, but it was obvious to her that his thoughts were far away.

Jessica still had Nicholas in tow when he glanced at his watch. "Wow!" he said. "I had no idea it was so late."

"Late?" Jessica said, pouting. "The party's just beginning."

"For you, maybe," he said, smiling. "But tomorrow's going to be a tough day for me. Even though it's Saturday, there are some VIPs coming in from Chicago to negotiate a deal with my father, and he expects me to be there."

15

"Couldn't you put it off?" Jessica cooed. "Just this once."

"I'm afraid not," Nicholas said. "Business is business."

"It's a shame to let it interfere with a good time, though," Jessica said.

"Sorry," Nicholas replied. "But that's the way it is. Anyway, Jessica, thanks for a wonderful evening. I really had a great time. And now I want to say good night to Elizabeth." He turned abruptly and walked away, leaving Jessica staring after him.

Todd stood beside Elizabeth on the opposite side of the room, his arm draped around her shoulder. "Tired?" he asked.

Elizabeth laughed and shook her head. "Should I be?"

"Playing hostess to a gang this size could wear anyone out," he said.

"But I love it," she insisted. "Besides, Jessica did most of the work."

Todd's eyebrow shot up. "Jessica?" he exclaimed. "Things sure have changed around here."

Ever loyal to her twin, Elizabeth protested, "You know Jessica does her best." Todd gave her a dubious look, and she quickly changed the subject to avoid an argument. "I'm not tired," she said, "but I'm practically dying of thirst."

"Want a root beer?"

"I'd love one." With a quick laugh she added, "But I'm not too tired to get it myself."

Todd silenced her with a quick kiss on her cheek. "One root beer, coming up." He hurried away in the direction of the buffet table.

Todd had not been gone five seconds when Elizabeth felt a hand on her shoulder. She whirled around in surprise. "Nicholas!" she exclaimed.

For the second time that evening, Nicholas was struck speechless. He looked so flustered that Elizabeth tried to put him at ease. "Going so soon?" she asked, noticing the jacket he was holding. "Couldn't you stay awhile longer?"

A look of relief crossed Nicholas's face. "I guess I can stay for a few more minutes," he said, gazing into Elizabeth's eyes. "But there's something I think I should tell you," he said, his voice shaking. "I know I've been following you around an awful lot tonight, and I want to apologize if I've bothered you."

Elizabeth smiled. "There's no need to apologize," she said sincerely. "I enjoyed meeting you."

"Me, too," Nicholas replied. "But I . . ." His voice trailed off, and Elizabeth sensed he was very uncomfortable about something.

"What's wrong?"

"Elizabeth—" Nicholas began, his face reddening, "I don't know how to tell you this. . . . I've never said anything so difficult in my life. But I guess it's best just to get it out into the

17

open, so here goes." He paused for a second and then said quickly, "Elizabeth, I think I'm falling in love with you!"

Elizabeth couldn't believe her ears. Nicholas Morrow in love with her? She caught her breath, then said, "But you don't even know me."

"That doesn't matter," Nicholas said. "I fell in love with you the minute I saw you."

"There in the moonlight?" Elizabeth asked. Nicholas nodded, and she laughed lightly. "Moonlight does strange things," she said. "You'll feel different tomorrow."

"I'll feel exactly the same," Nicholas insisted. "Try to understand."

"But, Nicholas . . ." Elizabeth paused, hating to hurt him. But she knew she had to tell the truth. "I already have a boyfriend. Todd Wilkins. You've met him."

"Todd Wilkins?" Nicholas asked. Everything fell into place. He was reminded of Regina's party and Todd's frantic search for Elizabeth. Jessica had disregarded Todd's questions about her sister's whereabouts until he finally pushed her into the Morrows' indoor pool. Nicholas also remembered how he had angrily asked Todd to leave, and he was embarrassed about the incident now. "Sure," he said. "Tall, good-looking. Doesn't he play basketball?"

"Yes. He's the best player on the team. Wait till you see him in the championship game."

Elizabeth's eyes shone with pride. "So you see—"

"I don't see anything," Nicholas said stubbornly.

Elizabeth sighed and took his hand. "I like you a lot. Really. But I don't think I could ever be in love with you."

"How can you tell? You don't even know me!"

"I know that, though," she said.

"Why?" he pressed her. "Am I really so unattractive?"

Elizabeth's eyes widened in astonishment. Didn't Nicholas Morrow know that he was great looking?

When Elizabeth said nothing, he repeated his question. "Am I really so unattractive? Frankenstein, maybe?" He screwed his face into a hideous mask. His eyes bulged, and his mouth twisted in a ghastly grin.

"Or Dracula?" He emitted a half-suppressed, bloodcurdling scream. "Or the Hunchback of Notre Dame?" He bent almost double, then shot his shoulders forward.

He was so ridiculous that Elizabeth burst out laughing. Then she looked at him critically. "Well, you don't have bolts coming out of your neck," she said, "so you can't be Frankenstein. And you don't have fangs, so you can't be Dracula."

"And I have two eyes, so—"

"So you can't be the one-eyed monster," Elizabeth said. She cocked her head to one side, studying him. "Let me see now . . ." Suddenly she snapped her fingers. "You must be Nicholas Morrow!" she said. "And you're really one of the most attractive guys I've ever met."

"You wouldn't be embarrassed to be seen with me?"

"Oh, I don't think so," she teased. "You may not be absolute perfection, of course, and you may even have a few minor character faults—"

"I used to bite my fingernails," Nicholas said, his eyes twinkling.

"See what I mean?" Elizabeth said brightly. "But otherwise?"

"Otherwise, I think you'll do," she said.

Nicholas's heart soared. "Then why not give me a chance? Come on, Elizabeth."

She shook her head, serious again. "I'm sorry, Nicholas," she said softly, "but I told you—I'm going out with Todd."

"But you're only sixteen," Nicholas argued. "That's too young to get tied up with just one person."

Just then Elizabeth heard Jessica saying goodbye to some kids at the front door. "I really have to say goodbye, too," Elizabeth said to Nicholas.

"No problem," he said. "I'll be waiting."

He smiled at her, but he looked so forlorn that Elizabeth promised, "I'll just be a minute." As she hurried off, she felt him gazing after her.

Elizabeth reached the door just as Robin

Wilson did, walking arm in arm with Allen Walters. "Liz," she said enthusiastically, "this party was fabulous."

Allen echoed her sentiments. "Sure was," he said.

Winston Egbert, following them, chimed in. "You can always count on a terrific time at the Wakefields'."

Elizabeth accepted the compliments graciously, giving Jessica all the credit. "My little sister really did a bang-up job this time," she said, referring to the fact that her twin was four minutes younger than she.

"Why not?" Jessica asked. "Nothing's too good for my big sister."

"We're glad to have you back, safe and sound," Enid Rollins said. She had lingered behind the others with her boyfriend, George Warren. "Oh, Liz!" she went on. "We were really scared for you!" She threw her arms around Elizabeth, giving her a bear hug.

"But it's over, Enid," Elizabeth said. "And I'm back here with all of you."

As her friends left, Elizabeth's thoughts returned to Nicholas Morrow and to his argument that she was too young to go steady. She'd heard the same thing a million times from her family since she'd gotten seriously involved with Todd. Elizabeth loved her parents dearly, and she knew they had her best interests at heart. But on this one thing she could never agree with them. She was so happy with Todd that she was sure there'd never be anyone else in her life. Not even Nicholas Morrow, she thought, as she closed the door behind the departing guests and went back to him.

She was afraid he'd bring up the subject once more, but this time Nicholas had a different argument. "You're just afraid, Elizabeth. That's the whole problem." His eyes met hers. "Isn't it?"

She shook her head. "Of course not."

"Then why don't you go out with me? Just once? That's all I'm asking. Just once!"

"I can't, Nicholas."

"You're not being fair. You don't even know me, yet you've already made a decision. Why?"

Elizabeth hesitated. Then she asked miserably, "What about Todd?"

"What about *me*?"

Her eyes filled with tears. It didn't seem fair that she should be held responsible for Nicholas's happiness. She wanted to be loyal to Todd, but she wanted to show compassion for Nicholas, too. Now she was confused about what to do. And on this of all days, one that was supposed to have been so happy.

She glanced around the room, holding back her tears. Then she focused her thoughts on Nicholas again as he urged, "Let me take you to dinner, Liz. Spend a couple of hours with me. That's really such a small favor."

The irony of it struck Elizabeth. Half the girls at Sweet Valley High would have sold their souls for a chance to have dinner with Nicholas Morrow, and here she was, hesitating.

Perhaps she ought to go out with Nicholas, Elizabeth thought. After all, he was new in town, and she did want to get to know him better. She certainly didn't want to make him feel uneasy by saying no. And it really wouldn't have to be a date, she rationalized. It could be more like dinner with a friend.

She relented at last, and agreed, giving him a bright smile. "OK, Nicholas, I'll have dinner with you."

She was rewarded with a smile so brilliant it put the sun to shame.

But once the words were out of her mouth, a new worry crossed Elizabeth's mind. Todd! She'd have to tell him about her dinner with Nicholas. There was no way out of *that*.

Not ask his permission, of course. Todd didn't own her any more than she owned him. But they'd always been honest with each other, and the decent thing would be to let him in on what was going on. She had no intention of deceiving Todd.

But how was she going to tell him? And when?

As soon as possible, Elizabeth decided.

She looked around the room. Todd was nowhere to be seen now, but her eyes lit on Jessica, talking to Randy Mason. Elizabeth wondered why, when half the time Jessica wouldn't give him even the time of day.

Elizabeth knew that Randy was sweet, but he wasn't Jessica's type. Lean and lanky, with horn-rimmed glasses and a shock of black hair that fell over his forehead, Randy wasn't bad-looking, but he certainly wasn't handsome. And around girls he was usually as tongue-tied as Nicholas Morrow had been earlier that evening. Still, he was a genius in math. And Elizabeth had heard that he was a whiz with computers.

Now, as snatches of their conversation floated by her, Elizabeth heard Jessica say, "I'm just fascinated by computers. Absolutely fascinated." Jessica fluttered her eyelashes and gave Randy one of her devastating smiles.

Elizabeth's jaw dropped. *Fascinated by computers?* Jessica had never even mentioned them before.

Then Elizabeth's heart sank as she realized that her twin had something up her sleeve. Elizabeth wasn't sure what it was, but she was certain that it would suit only Jessica. *Oh, Jess,* Elizabeth thought, *how could you?*

But it was hard for Elizabeth to be annoyed with Jessica for long. In fact, she even felt a tiny pang of wistful envy. If only she could be more like her twin, she thought, life would be so much simpler. Then she wouldn't have to worry about hurting Nicholas's feelings, or Todd's, either.

She wasn't like Jessica, though. So she sternly ordered herself to face facts. She'd have to tell Todd, even if she was certain he wouldn't like it. Still, if he loved and trusted her—*and he does*, she told herself—he'd understand.

Elizabeth was so deep in thought that she didn't hear what Nicholas said next. She looked up and saw him regarding her expectantly. "I'm sorry," she said, smiling. "I guess I was daydreaming."

"That's OK," Nicholas said as they started walking to the door. "I just wanted to know if next Saturday would be all right."

Elizabeth shook her head. "No good. That's Todd's night. We have a standing date."

"Sunday, then?"

Elizabeth thought for a moment, then nodded. "That's Todd's mother's birthday," she said. "He'll be spending the day with her."

"So?" Nicholas prodded as they reached the end of the hall.

"Sunday would be OK," Elizabeth said.

"Sunday," Nicholas said, opening the door. Before he stepped through it, he planted a kiss on her cheek. "That's great. And I'll call you Wednesday night, OK?"

"Yes," Elizabeth said. "Call me on Wednesday." But as soon as she'd said this, she was gripped by a terrible premonition. No good would come of this date, she thought. No good at all!

Yet she'd made a promise, and she'd have to keep it. Elizabeth could only hope that her fears were groundless.

Three

Nicholas went down the path and climbed into his Jeep. He started the motor, then leaned out to wave to Elizabeth. "Sunday," he said, grinning from ear to ear. "It's going to be a great day!"

Elizabeth waved back, wondering just what she'd gotten herself into. Then she closed the door and went to look for Todd.

As she walked into the living room, where The Droids were packing up their equipment, Elizabeth saw that Randy Mason was still talking to Jessica. Listening to her, rather.

Jessica had moved closer to him, and her head was bent to his. "Computers just seem so complicated," she said, pouting. "I just don't know how anyone can understand them. I don't even know a byte from a nibble!"

To Elizabeth's dismay, Randy seemed completely taken in by Jessica's line. He gave her a shy but happy smile. Then he said, "They're not really so complicated, Jessica. Actually they're pretty easy once you understand how they work."

"Easy for you, maybe," Jessica said. "But for me . . . " She shook her head, pouting again. "When it comes to things like that, I'm an absolute airhead. Why, I even have trouble with math." She gave a self-deprecating little laugh. "I'll tell you a secret," she said. "I had trouble learning the multiplication table."

Randy laughed. "Oh, Jessica! Anyone can learn math. And anyone can learn about computers!"

"I wish *I* could," Jessica said, sighing.

Randy swallowed hard. He looked at Jessica for a long time. Finally he cleared his throat and said in a husky voice, "Well, if you really *want* to learn about computers, maybe I could teach you!"

Jessica's eyes lit up, and she clapped her hands together in delight. "Oh, Randy!" she said. "Could you? Do you really think you could?"

"Sure," he said, blushing a deep, dark red. But he was grinning, too. "Would you like me to, Jessica?"

"Like it?" she caroled. "Oh, Randy, there's absolutely nothing in this whole wide world I'd like more! Oh, Randy . . ." Jessica moved still closer to him as Elizabeth walked out of the room and headed through the dining room toward the kitchen to find Todd. He wasn't there, but Elizabeth, feeling guilty for not spending more time with her guests, stopped to talk to Olivia Davidson, the *Oracle*'s arts editor, and her boyfriend Roger Barrett. Then Elizabeth wandered out to the patio.

She spotted Todd almost at once. He was sitting on one of the deck chairs drawn up around the pool. His arms hung at his sides like lead, and he was snapping his fingers aimlessly. Elizabeth knew at once she was in for trouble.

She went over to him. "Todd," she said, tousling his chestnut-colored hair. "What are you doing out here all alone?"

He mumbled an unintelligible answer.

"You know," Elizabeth went on, "I hardly had a chance to talk to you all evening."

"I wouldn't say 'all evening,' " Todd said, speaking at last. But his tone was sullen. "You just didn't have a chance to talk to me after Nicholas Morrow showed up."

"Oh, Todd," Elizabeth said soothingly. "Nicholas is new in town. And you know how hard it is for a stranger to adjust to a new place."

"So you're making it easy for him by acting like the lady from the Welcome Wagon!"

Elizabeth's quick smile was answered by a grudging one from Todd. But then he complained again. "Why was he hanging around you all evening?"

"Oh, Todd! I don't think he was."

"No? He never let you out of his sight!"

Elizabeth touched Todd's shoulder gently.

"He danced with me a couple of times," she protested quietly. "Then he went off with Jessica."

"Then Jessica *dragged* him off," Todd said. "But maybe they deserve each other."

Elizabeth was always sensitive to such comments about Jessica, and she could tell the moment she heard it just how upset Todd was with *her*.

"Todd Wilkins! You're jealous!" she reproved him gently, then brushed a kiss across the top of his head.

"Can you blame me?" Todd asked morosely. "Nicholas is rich and good-looking, so he thinks he owns the world. And now he's going after the most wonderful girl in Sweet Valley, who's supposed to be in love with me. At least that was what I thought."

"I *am* in love with you, Todd," Elizabeth said simply and sincerely.

Todd smiled gratefully at Elizabeth, then pulled her down beside him, putting his arm around her. His voice sounded relieved as he said, "I guess I knew that all the time, Liz. Just the way I know I can always trust you." He planted a kiss firmly on her mouth.

As she felt his lips on hers, Elizabeth's resolve to tell Todd about Nicholas evaporated. Now wasn't the time, she told herself. Not after Todd had been so upset. In a few days she'd be able to make it all seem as casual as it was. With that in mind, Elizabeth walked arm in arm with Todd back to the party.

The remaining guests left a short time later, but Todd lingered behind. At the door he kissed Elizabeth once again, a long, passionate kiss as they said good night. Then he got into his car and drove off.

Elizabeth watched Todd's car until it disappeared. Then she went back into the living room. Mr. and Mrs. Wakefield had gone to bed, and the living room was deserted now except for Jessica, who had curled up in a corner of the couch.

Almost automatically, Elizabeth began to pick up the empty glasses that littered the place. "Jessica, give me a hand," she said to her twin. "This place looks like a tornado hit it."

"Sure, Liz," Jessica said, remaining seated.

"Come on," Elizabeth said.

"In a minute. But I want to talk to you first."

"Can't we talk while we clean up this place? I'm tired."

"I guess we could."

Jessica picked up a crumpled paper napkin and followed her twin, who had both hands filled with glasses, into the kitchen.

Jessica halfheartedly started putting things away in the kitchen while Elizabeth grabbed a tray and headed back to pick up the remaining dishes. When she staggered into the kitchen, carrying the heavily loaded tray, Jessica was sitting on a stool. She looked up at Elizabeth and exclaimed fervently, "You're the only one who really understands me!"

"OK, Jessica. I understand you," Elizabeth said as she began to load the dishwasher. "So what is it?"

There was no answer, and Elizabeth turned to look at her twin. Jessica's face was transfigured with an expression of utter bliss. "Well?" Elizabeth asked.

"Liz . . ." Jessica began, then paused dramatically. Elizabeth went back to loading the dishwasher but stopped short when Jessica announced, "I'm in love."

So what else is new? Elizabeth asked herself. Aloud she said, "And who's the lucky guy?"

"Oh, Liz! You'd never believe me." Jessica sighed.

"Maybe yes, maybe no," Elizabeth said. "But I can't really tell until I know who it is, can I?"

"No, I guess you're right about that," Jessica admitted. "It's Nicholas Morrow!"

"Nicholas Morrow!" Elizabeth exclaimed.

"That's right," Jessica said happily. "And, Liz, I'm sure he's in love with me!"

"Well, if you say so," Elizabeth murmured under her breath.

Elizabeth took her mind off Jessica for a while by scraping plates and rinsing silver. Then she asked, "If you're in love with Nicholas and Nicholas is in love with you, then what was all that talk with Randy Mason about?"

"Oh, that?" Jessica said with a shrug. "Isn't it obvious?"

"Not to me," Elizabeth said, frowning.

"Oh, Liz!" Jessica sighed. "How can you be so utterly, absolutely dense? Randy knows all about computers. And the Morrows are in the computer business. And Nicholas is taking a year off before college to learn about them—"

"I know all that," Elizabeth said. "So what's next?"

"Well, like I said, it's obvious. Nicholas could hardly care about someone—I mean *really* care—about someone who didn't share his interests."

"Those interests being computers?"

Jessica danced across the room and hugged her sister. "Liz, your powers of deduction are absolutely incredible," she said.

Elizabeth felt her heart slide down to her toes. She'd been curious before. But now she understood what Jessica was up to. Jessica wasn't interested in Randy at all. She was only using him to snag Nicholas.

Then another thought struck Elizabeth: How could she possibly talk to Jessica about her own problem with Nicholas? It had been at the back of her mind that Jessica could help her work things out. But there was no way she could confide in her sister now. No way! Not when the boy Jessica was mad about was in love with *her*.

Elizabeth went into the dining room, Jessica at her heels. She began to sweep up the crumbs from the table, but all the while the question of whether or not she should go out with Nicholas whirled in her brain. She was so preoccupied with the problem that she missed most of what her twin was saying.

But Elizabeth came to with a start when Jessica uttered, "He's the most gorgeous guy I've ever met." She put her hand to her heart and sighed.

When Elizabeth made no answer, Jessica rambled on. "Oh, Liz! Where's he been all my life? Here I am, sixteen years old, and for the first time, the *very* first time, I've met a regular . . . regular . . ."

"Adonis?" Elizabeth queried.

"Adonis? I don't know exactly."

"He was the Greek god we learned about in English class," Elizabeth said.

"Then that's what he is!" Jessica exulted. "Nicholas Morrow. A regular Adonis. Don't you think so, too?"

"Oh, sure," Elizabeth said, with a notable lack of enthusiasm.

But Jessica was too wrapped up in her own dreams to notice. "Elizabeth," she said, dropping to the couch, "Nicholas Morrow is the guy I've been waiting for practically forever."

The bowl of popcorn Elizabeth was holding went crashing to the floor. As she bent to pick up the scattered kernels, Jessica went on. "Oh, Liz! Can you imagine what a date with Nicholas would be like?"

The irony of Jessica's words swept over Elizabeth like a wave. Jessica was dreaming of a date with Nicholas, but Elizabeth was actually going to go out with him! How would Jessica react when she found out about Elizabeth's dinner date with Nicholas? As she picked the last kernel of popcorn off the floor, Elizabeth realized that she couldn't tell Jessica about her date; she would have to keep it a secret. She knew her twin's temper too well to risk an explosion. Elizabeth would tell Todd about Nicholas but not Jessica. What her twin didn't know wouldn't hurt her, Elizabeth thought. *And Jessica will never know*, she vowed.

As for Nicholas, he'd have the chance he'd asked for. But she'd make sure that their dinner together would be very quiet and very private. Quick, too. They'd go to some restaurant where there'd be no chance whatever of running into anyone they knew. And once dinner was over, she'd leave Nicholas and come straight home.

Elizabeth knew he might be hurt, and she was truly sorry about it. But wasn't she giving him what he'd said he wanted? Wasn't she giving him at least a shot?

Four

Elizabeth waited for Jessica in the little red Fiat Spider. Mrs. Wakefield would stay at home that week, taking a vacation from her job as an interior designer, and had given Elizabeth permission to drive the car to and from school. After what seemed like a couple of hundred years, Elizabeth tooted the horn.

At the sound, Jessica tore out of the Wakefield house and climbed in beside her sister. She was wearing a pale-blue miniskirt and a matching V-neck sweater. "Do you think I could wear this outfit if I went on a date with Nicholas?" she asked, smoothing down the skirt.

"Is Nicholas Morrow the only thing on your mind?" Elizabeth said, bridling at the mention of his name. She glanced anxiously at her watch, then backed carefully out of the driveway.

Jessica followed her glance. "You're always in such a hurry, Liz," she said. "Why don't you do what I did? Throw away that ticking little time

35

bomb on your wrist. It doesn't really matter if we get to school after the first bell rings."

"Not to you, maybe," Elizabeth said. "But it does to me."

"Maybe if they'd let *me* drive . . ." The "they" was a reference to the twins' parents, Ned and Alice Wakefield, who'd forbidden Jessica the use of the car because of the numerous traffic tickets she'd received in the past.

"But they won't let you drive," Elizabeth said in a level voice. "So if you want to ride, you'll have to come with me. And you'd better be ready when I am."

"Oh, Liz! The way you talk, you might as well be someone's grandmother or something. I really don't know what's the matter with you," Jessica said primly.

"There's absolutely nothing the matter with me," Elizabeth answered, struggling to control her temper. "For your information—"

"For *yours*," Jessica said, "you're edgy all the time. Honestly, you act like some sort of minor-league monster. I just hope we don't run into Nicholas. You'd probably scare him away."

"There's absolutely nothing the matter with me," Elizabeth repeated angrily.

"It may look like that from where you sit. As for me"—Jessica opened her purse and pulled out her lip gloss, touching up her makeup, which was already close to perfect—"it seems that every time I so much as mention Nicholas Morrow you practically snap my head off."

Elizabeth bent forward, concentrating on the road. Jessica continued to babble, but Elizabeth tuned her out. She was still so worried about her upcoming date with Nicholas that she couldn't think of anything else.

The same questions kept popping into her mind, and she'd begun to think of herself as some kind of phonograph record, stuck in the same groove and spinning around and around and around. How was she going to tell Todd about Nicholas? And what if someone found out that she'd gone to dinner with him and told Jessica? She'd be wiped out.

Elizabeth hoped her twin would forget Nicholas by then. At present, though, it seemed to Elizabeth that he was all Jessica talked about. The night before she'd asked, "Elizabeth, do you think I should call Nicholas?"

"If you want to," Elizabeth had replied, knowing full well that Jessica wasn't really asking for advice and would do whatever she wanted to. Later, when Elizabeth was in the bathroom that connected her room with Jessica's, she overheard her sister speaking to him. "You're so smart, Nicholas," she gushed. "Why, you'll probably go to one of those Ivy League schools back East, won't you? Or maybe even to MIT. Isn't that where people go to learn about electronics?"

Now, as Elizabeth drove to school, Jessica announced, "You know, Elizabeth, I'm meeting him after school."

37

Elizabeth's thoughts had been wandering. Now she jerked upright in her seat and gave Jessica a startled look. "Nicholas Morrow?" she asked.

"Oh, Liz," Jessica said, pouting, "don't you ever listen to a word I say? I just told you, I have some serious business with Randy Mason after school, so I won't be riding home with you."

"That's OK with me," Elizabeth said. *But poor Randy*, she added to herself. For him it couldn't mean anything but trouble.

Randy was waiting for Jessica under the big Romanesque clock that was the pride of Sweet Valley High. He glanced around anxiously, then checked his watch. Five minutes later he checked his watch again. When he finally spotted Jessica ambling toward him, a look of relief spread across his face. He waved, then rushed forward to meet her.

Jessica gave him a carefully calculated bright smile. Then she began to chatter at breakneck speed. "Oh, Randy! It's just absolutely wonderful that you're taking all this time and trouble just to show me how computers work."

She seemed so ecstatic that Randy's heart almost stopped. His face turned scarlet, and he stammered in embarrassment. "Gee, Jessica, it's really nothing."

"Randy!" Jessica stared at him in amazement. "It isn't! *It isn't*."

She edged close to him, letting her head fall

on his shoulder. He squirmed and moved away, more embarrassed than he'd ever been in his life. "Come on, then," he said, swallowing hard. "We'd better get started."

Jessica laughed to herself. Randy really was falling for her act. Imagine his thinking she was interested in him! Didn't Randy know that he was a nerd? And that she only wanted to learn about computers to impress Nicholas? Otherwise she wouldn't give Randy a second glance.

But Jessica needed him at the moment, so she jumped into the battered old jalopy Randy passed off as a car. As he drove toward his house, she shot him an adoring look. Though her mind was on Nicholas, she kept up a running conversation. "It's so ridiculous," she insisted. "Here I am living in the twentieth century, and I don't know a single, solitary thing about computers."

"Come on, Jessica. That's the way a lot of people talk. You'd be surprised at how much you know already."

"Randy! I told you I can barely add two plus two."

"That doesn't make any difference to the computer," Randy said stoutly.

"Well, whatever the computer thinks, I know what I know." Jessica smiled sheepishly. "Or what I don't know."

Randy pulled up in front of a split-level house that was almost exactly like the Wakefields'. "Let's find out," he said.

They went inside, and Randy led Jessica to his room. There was a bed against one wall, with a chair beside it. There was a dresser, too. But most of the room was taken up with what Randy called his "work center"—a computer, a terminal, a printer.

"Pretty terrific, isn't it?" He patted the computer proudly, the way Bruce Patman patted the hood of his Porsche. Jessica wondered if Randy polished his computer every day too.

"Terrific," Jessica agreed, forcing a smile. "But I still haven't got any idea how to work it. I mean it seems so terribly difficult. All those keys. And those little gadgets. And that TV screen. How on earth can you tell what they're for?"

"It's easy, Jessica. Here, let me show you." Randy switched on the computer, then got out a diskette and held it out for Jessica's inspection. "This is called a floppy disk," he said.

"Really?" Jessica opened her eyes wide in pretended astonishment. "I don't think I've ever seen one before," she fibbed.

"No?" Randy looked so surprised that Jessica was afraid she'd overdone it this time.

But to her relief, he hadn't caught on. He was so completely wrapped up in his explanations that he hardly noticed her. It was the first time in her life, Jessica thought, she'd ever had to compete with a *machine*!

"You insert the disk like this," he told her.

Jessica nodded. "Oh, I see."

"Sure you do. You're intelligent, Jessica.

You can do anything you put your mind to," Randy said with genuine admiration.

Jessica lowered her eyes modestly. "I don't think so," she said. She was bored stiff, listening to Randy. Still, if she learned enough to impress Nicholas and get him to ask her out, it was worth her while. She'd do anything for Nicholas!

Randy had no idea what was on Jessica's mind. He just went on, tossing around words and expressions like "CP/M" and "FORTRAN" and "sysgen." Then he suggested that Jessica run a program herself.

She did it so easily that Randy was delighted. "See!" he said, chortling. "I told you you could. It hasn't taken you any time at all, and see how much you've picked up."

Jessica gave Randy a smile so bright it almost blinded him. "I could never have done it without you," she said. "You make it so fascinating. I'll bet if *you* were teaching math at Sweet Valley High, I'd never fail," she added, piling on the compliments.

From behind his glasses, Randy's dark eyes glowed. "I could help you with your math," he suggested hopefully.

"No one could," Jessica said with an earthshaking sigh. She shook her head, thinking of her problems in that department. "Absolutely no one."

"Put that back!" Elizabeth snapped as

Jessica emerged from Elizabeth's closet, holding her new turquoise jumpsuit. "That's mine!"

"I *know* it's yours, Liz," Jessica said, walking over to Elizabeth's mirror. She held the suit out in front of her. "It wouldn't be in your closet if it wasn't yours."

"It looks to me as if it's going to end up in *your* closet," Elizabeth said. She was curled up on her bed with a book open in front of her. Looking down at it, she realized she'd been staring at the same page for at least ten minutes.

She clapped the book shut and tossed it onto the floor. "What do you want with it, anyway?"

"I want to wear it," Jessica said, tossing her head.

Elizabeth groaned. "That's what I thought."

"Don't you think it would look absolutely great on me?" Jessica asked brightly.

"It would be OK," Elizabeth admitted, "*If* I let you wear it."

"You've always let me borrow your clothes before," Jessica argued.

"That was before," Elizabeth muttered. "It might not be now, though."

Jessica was the picture of despair as she hung the jumpsuit in Elizabeth's closet. Then she spun around to face her sister. "What's wrong with you, Liz?" she asked.

Elizabeth shook her head. "I don't know," she said listlessly. Her eyes misted over. "I'm sorry, Jess," she said. "I didn't mean to act like that. Of course you can wear the jumpsuit. It'll probably look better on you than it does on me, anyway."

"Oh, Liz!" Jessica threw her arms around her twin. "You're the kindest, most generous, best-hearted person in the whole wide world."

Elizabeth gave her sister a sickly smile. "Aren't you getting a little carried away?" she said.

"It's true," Jessica insisted. "And you're the best writer too. That last story you wrote for *The Oracle* had everyone raving."

"Thanks," Elizabeth said.

The story was about the computer Kurt Morrow, Nicholas and Regina's father, had presented to Sweet Valley High. It was to be used to keep track of the students' grades. According to Elizabeth's article, "This new piece of equipment will be a boon to the staff and administrators. No more lost records. No more inaccurate records. No more delays in getting out grades. Sweet Valley High is cashing in on the wave of the future!"

Mr. Collins, the faculty adviser for the newspaper, had been as enthusiastic about it as Jessica. "Your best yet," he'd assured Elizabeth, hoping his praise would snap her out of the blue mood she'd been in.

She'd smiled bleakly. "Thanks, Mr. Collins. I'm glad you liked it." Then, reminded still another time of her date with Nicholas Morrow, she'd gone back to brooding over it.

The story reminded Jessica of Nicholas, too. And the line about no delays in getting grades out reminded her of her own failing math grade. Elizabeth's "wave of the future," she thought miserably, was about to sweep her off the cheerleading squad, since one of the cheerleading rules was that anyone who failed a subject was barred from the squad.

Jessica had practically given up hope when she picked up *The Sweet Valley News* later that afternoon and read another article about computers. There were kids known as hackers, it said, who'd been plugging into computer terminals all over the state. It was even suspected that some had altered data stored in the computers.

She wondered who those kids were and what they were like. Geniuses in math, probably. And nerds, too, like Randy Mason.

Then an idea hit her so hard she reeled. If *they* could plug into computers, couldn't Randy?

She didn't know. She didn't even know if she'd dare to ask him. Still, it was worth a try. And it certainly was worth keeping her date with Randy that night instead of begging off with a story about having a splitting headache.

She was glad she did when he picked her up in his rattling old car and drove her to the Dairi Burger. "You know, you're really pretty terrific," he said as he dug into his fried clams.

Jessica laughed lightly. "I'll bet you say that to all the girls," she told him.

"No, I don't, Jessica. Fact is," he said, reaching for the ketchup, "I don't go out with many girls."

"No!" Jessica faked a surprised look.

Randy fell for it. "No, really. I've never even had a girlfriend. Would you believe that?"

I sure would, Jessica said to herself. But she shook her head and said aloud, "That's really hard to imagine!"

Randy was so taken by Jessica's act that he forgot he was pouring ketchup on his clams. By the time Jessica pointed to his plate, the bottle was half-empty, and the clams looked like a scene from a horror movie. Randy looked down at the mess and shrugged. "Oh, well," he said cheerfully. "I like ketchup."

He picked up a french fry, dipped it into the ketchup, and chewed on it thoughtfully. "What I meant when I said you were so terrific," he explained, "was the way you caught on to all that stuff I was telling you about computers."

Jessica shook her head and stared at the table. "But I hardly know a thing," she said demurely.

"That isn't so, Jessica!"

"Yes, it is!" She sighed to signal her despair. But out of the corner of her eye she watched Randy's face.

It was ablaze with happiness and love. Jessica tossed her head triumphantly.

Now that Randy was ripe for the picking, she moved ahead. "You've been wonderful to me, Randy," she whispered.

Randy scratched the nape of his neck. "Gee, Jessica. You know I'd do anything for you."

"Would you?" She leaned across the table and looked at him earnestly.

"Sure. Is there something you want?"

"There is." Jessica looked down and fiddled with her fork. "But I hate to ask you."

"Hey! I just told you I'd do anything."

"Even *you* probably couldn't do anything about this."

"I could try," Randy offered.

"To teach me math? And get me through this term?"

Randy suddenly straightened up and looked very self-assured. "Is that all? Sure, I could do that. Results guaranteed, too."

Once again, Jessica exulted inwardly. But to Randy she said morosely, "It's much too late for that."

"You'd be surprised." Randy thrust his chest out so far Jessica thought he'd split his T-shirt. "Want to go over your math with me Thursday?"

Jessica's look promised eternal gratitude. "Could we, Randy?"

"Sure," he said. "What time?"

Jessica shrugged. "I don't know. Why don't you give me a call tomorrow, and we'll set up a time?"

"Sounds good to me," he said, mopping up more of the ketchup with a soggy french fry.

Five

"Oh, Liz, you're the sweetest sister in the world," Jessica babbled. "Driving me down to the mall like this. It's so mean of Mom and Dad not to let me have the car."

Jessica's woeful cry fell on deaf ears. Elizabeth had heard it time and time again. Her answer was to remind her sister that they could spend only a short time shopping. "Remember, Jess, we have to study tonight."

"*You* have to study," Jessica retorted. If Elizabeth wanted to bury her head in a book, that was her problem. As for Jessica, she had better things to do.

Elizabeth deftly eased the little Fiat into an open space. The twins got out and walked toward the shopping center.

"Cara Walker says the dresses that just came in at Foxy Mama's are fabulous," Jessica said as they strolled toward one of her favorite shops. She came to a dead stop in front of the window.

"Oh," she squealed, "did you ever see anything so gorgeous?"

Elizabeth had to agree that the low-cut, pale-pink dress in the window was sensational. She could imagine exactly how it would look on Jessica.

The two girls were eyeing the dress so intently that they were startled when a voice called out, "Well, if it isn't the Wakefield twins." Spinning around, they saw Nicholas Morrow standing before them.

Elizabeth's heart leaped into her throat. *Oh, no!* she thought. *What if Nicholas says something about dinner on Sunday?* But she realized that the situation was out of her hands. She could only remain calm and hope that Nicholas wouldn't mention their date.

Jessica, however, took the chance encounter in her usual stride. "Nicholas Morrow! We didn't expect to see you here."

"I didn't expect to see you. This must be my lucky day," he said, glancing at Elizabeth.

"Why, thank you, Nicholas," Jessica said coyly. "But I thought you'd be at work now. Or do you get time off for good behavior?"

"I manage to escape sometimes. Not often, though," Nicholas answered, grinning.

"Oh, Nicholas," Jessica gushed, putting on her most dazzling smile. "I think it's wonderful that you work all day. But then, computers are just too fascinating for words."

Elizabeth gulped, but Nicholas agreed. "It is

48

an interesting business. The 'wave of the future,' as Elizabeth wrote in that article."

"And you're part of that wave."

Even for Jessica, this was overdoing it, Elizabeth thought, still saying nothing.

Nicholas laughed. "More like a ripple, actually. Still, it's pretty exciting."

His eyes were still on Elizabeth, but Jessica didn't seem to notice. "Nicholas, you're just so funny," she gushed. "Don't you think so, Liz?"

"Yes," Elizabeth replied, blushing.

"Well, I've got to go," Nicholas said. "But I'll see you again, won't I?" he asked, directing his question to Elizabeth.

"Of course, Nicholas. I'm looking forward to it," Jessica answered, her voice filled with excitement. "Just call me anytime."

Elizabeth breathed a sigh of relief as Nicholas walked away. She was off the hook—for the moment.

"Oh, Liz," Jessica trilled. "Nicholas Morrow is the most adorable guy I've ever met. And he wants to go out with me! Isn't that wonderful? Every girl in Sweet Valley will be jealous." Then, turning back to the store window, she said, "Liz, I think I'm going to buy that dress. I'll just have to have something spectacular to wear when Nicholas Morrow takes me out."

It was Wednesday night, and even though Elizabeth was expecting Nicholas to call, the shrill ring of the telephone startled her on the stairs. "I'll get it," she said, sprinting for the phone in her room.

Jessica was hot on her heels. "It's for me," she yelled, trying to elbow Elizabeth aside.

But Elizabeth was too quick for her. She picked up the telephone and said hello, expecting to hear Nicholas's voice and wondering what she could say to him with Jessica, all ears now, practically on top of her.

"Hi!" The voice that came over the line was strange to Elizabeth. "Could I speak to Jessica, please?"

"Oh, sure!"

"Who is it?" Jessica mouthed.

"I don't know," she mouthed back, handing the phone to Jessica.

"Hello?" Jessica said. "Oh, Randy!" There was a pause, then Jessica said, "Tomorrow afternoon? That would be just perfect! Listen, I'm on Liz's extension. Hang on a second and I'll pick it up in my room." She handed the phone to Elizabeth and raced out of the room.

Elizabeth waited to hang up until she heard Jessica pick up. *Poor Randy*, she thought. He seemed like such a nice guy, and she hated to see him get hurt. But she was sure he'd be crushed when Jessica dropped him, as she was certain to do.

Elizabeth walked over to her bureau and stood in front of it, staring at herself in the mirror hanging above it. There were little worry lines on her forehead. Elizabeth tried to rub them out with the back of her hand. The lines disappeared, but her doubts about dinner on Sunday kept plaguing her. She still hadn't said a word to Todd about her date with Nicholas. And she was terrified that Jessica would catch on and go into one of her Technicolor rages. Elizabeth knew she should never have agreed to go out with Nicholas, yet here she was, waiting for his phone call.

"Oh, stop it!" she ordered herself. "Everything will be all right!"

But what if it wasn't?

Elizabeth started pacing across the room. She picked up a book, leafed through it, and put it down. With nothing better to do to pass the time, she examined her nails. She thought a different shade of polish might change her mood, as it did Jessica's.

She walked into the bathroom and regarded the bottles carefully arranged on her vanity. She wasn't the least bit tempted by any of the colors. Sighing, she returned to her room.

She began to wander around her room again. After she'd circled it a couple of times, still trying to find something to occupy her, Elizabeth gave up. There was nothing to do, she decided, but to sit and wait. And try not to bite her nails.

She was sitting cross-legged on her bed, listening to the ticking of the tiny clock on the table beside it when the telephone jangled again. "I've got it," she called, picking up her extension on the first ring.

She made sure that Jessica hadn't picked up, too. When there wasn't so much as a peep out of her, Elizabeth cautiously said, "Hello?"

"Hello, Liz?" Elizabeth recognized the voice even before he said, "This is Nicholas Morrow."

"Hi, Nicholas. How are you?"

"Fine. How are you?"

"Couldn't be better," Elizabeth said. "It sure was a coincidence, running into you in the mall this afternoon."

"Sure was," Nicholas agreed. "And it was the first time I've been out on my own all week. I guess Jessica told you I had to show a lot of VIPs around."

"That must have kept you busy."

"I didn't really mind. The last few days have practically flown by."

"Well, you'll have some free time now," Elizabeth said.

"I sort of wish I didn't. Now the days are going to crawl until Sunday comes." Nicholas paused, then asked in a quiet voice, "Is our date still on?"

About a million butterflies took off from somewhere in the pit of Elizabeth's stomach and began to swarm around. She took a deep breath, hoping they'd go back to wherever they had come from. At the same time she heard a little voice at the back of her mind telling her to say no.

But she'd made a promise, and she felt she had to keep it. "Yes," she said at last, in a low voice.

"Dinner?"

"Dinner," Elizabeth agreed.

"That's great!" Nicholas said. Then he asked, "Is there any special restaurant you'd like to go to?"

"No," Elizabeth said. "I can't think of anyplace."

There were a hundred restaurants she could think of that she *didn't* want to go to. They were places where she might run into someone she knew, one of the kids from school, or even their parents. If anyone recognized her, it would be all over Sweet Valley before morning that she had been out with Nicholas Morrow. The very first to hear that bit of especially juicy gossip would have to be Jessica.

"How does the Côte d'Or sound to you?" Nicholas asked. "That is if you don't mind a drive of an hour or so."

Mind! Would she mind winning first prize in the lottery? "That's perfect," Elizabeth said, not hiding her enthusiasm. "I'd love to go there, Nicholas."

"I hope you'll like it," he said. "It's supposed to be good."

Expensive, too. Elizabeth had read something about it in some magazine. "Exquisite," they had called it. "The specialties are . . ." and

53

a long list followed. After that were prices that had made Elizabeth blink.

It was the perfect place for her: one that was far away from Sweet Valley and that no one else she knew could even afford, at least none of the kids.

As all that flashed through her mind, she heard Nicholas ask, "Shall I pick you up Sunday evening?"

"Oh, no!"

"I understand. I'd love to drive you over myself, but if you'd rather meet me there . . ."

"I'd rather meet you there," Elizabeth said firmly.

"About six-thirty? Would that be all right?"

"Six-thirty would be just fine," Elizabeth said.

After she'd hung up, it occurred to Elizabeth that she'd have to wear something suitable for her date. The casual outfits that were perfect when she went out with Todd would hardly do for dinner at the Côte d'Or.

Mentally she sorted through her wardrobe. Nothing seemed right. Her mouth twitched in a wry smile as she remembered the red velour skirt and the white blouse Jessica had laid out for her to wear to the party at the Morrows' the night she was kidnapped. In comparison to the sexy outfit Jessica herself wore, Elizabeth would have looked practically middle-aged.

So that was out. But Elizabeth, certain she had something appropriate in her closet, put all thoughts of what she would wear out of her mind. She couldn't stop worrying, though, about going out with Nicholas. She sighed. Now that the arrangements were all made, the fat was in the fire. She could only hope it didn't flare up and burn her!

Elizabeth drove home alone from school early Thursday afternoon. School had been let out at noon for a teachers' conference. Ordinarily Elizabeth would have been thankful for the free time, but now it seemed she only had extra hours to worry about her date with Nicholas Morrow. She still hadn't told Todd about her plans, and now she wasn't even sure she should. She needed to talk to someone, and she decided to call Enid Rollins as soon as she got home. After all, Enid was her best friend, and Elizabeth had always been able to count on her for good advice.

She dashed into the house as soon as she'd parked the car, went to her room, and picked up her telephone, hoping Enid would be home. When Enid picked up on the second ring, Elizabeth sighed with relief. "Oh, Enid!" she burst out. "I just have to talk to you!"

"What's up, Liz? You sound as if the roof caved in."

"It could," Elizabeth said, with a catch in her voice.

Enid waited for Elizabeth to go on. When

nothing came but the hum of the open line, she suggested gently, "Maybe I can help. But first you'll have to tell me what's the matter."

Suddenly Elizabeth poured out the whole story. "So Nicholas asked me for a date," she concluded, "Sunday night."

"Nicholas Morrow!" Enid said in surprise. Then she asked dubiously, "Are you going?"

"I don't want to," Elizabeth said. "But Nicholas absolutely insisted. At first I thought I'd tell Todd, but now I'm afraid to. And I'm also scared that Jessica will find out somehow."

There was a long pause. Elizabeth, knowing Enid so well, could almost see the look on her face as she considered the situation. Then Enid said, "I can understand about Todd. But Jessica?"

"She's in love with him," Elizabeth said, her voice quivering.

"I should have known," Enid said derisively. "Doesn't she fall for every handsome guy in town? And Nicholas is rich, too."

Elizabeth knew Enid was no fan of Jessica's, and this time she ignored Enid's criticism. There were more important things to discuss.

Enid went on. "Don't worry, Liz. She'll forget him as soon as someone else comes along."

"Not this time. She thinks Nicholas is in love with her."

"Is he?"

"No," Elizabeth said, choking back a sob. "He says he's in love with me."

There was a stunned silence. Then Enid said, "Hmmm. The plot thickens."

"You've got it," Elizabeth said. "And I don't know what to do. I don't want to hurt Jessica or Todd. But I don't want to hurt Nicholas, either. And I've promised I'd go."

"Oh, Liz!" Enid said sympathetically. There was another long pause as she considered her friend's predicament. Finally she said, "I think you'll just have to go out with Nicholas, Liz. And keep your fingers crossed and hope that Jessica doesn't find out. But I also think it's important that you tell Todd about this. Todd's understanding."

"Not when it comes to Nicholas Morrow," Elizabeth said glumly. "But you're right, Enid. It's only fair to tell Todd." In her heart, though, Elizabeth knew it would be one of the most difficult things she'd ever have to do.

The hands of the Romanesque clock were at five minutes past twelve as Randy approached it and settled back to wait for Jessica. Fifteen minutes later she strolled slowly toward him. "Hi," she said, greeting Randy casually. "I guess I'm late. Sorry about that."

"You don't have to apologize," Randy said, smiling shyly. "I know what it's like to be tied up with something really important."

As they walked to the parking lot, Randy shot Jessica an adoring look. Then they climbed into his car, and he started the motor. "What's the problem with the math?" he asked as he put the car into gear and maneuvered it into traffic.

"I just can't understand anything about it!"

"It's simple," Randy said. "You'll see. Gee, Jessica, if you can figure out how to run a computer the way you did, math should be easy for you."

Jessica moved a little closer to him. "But working on the computer was *fun*," she said. "And math is so dull."

"Math's fun! It's a kind of game, like chess!"

"If it is," Jessica said dubiously, "let's play."

They reached the Mason house and went to Randy's room. "OK, let's see your book," Randy said.

Jessica held it at arm's length. Randy chuckled. "It won't bite," he said. "And once you understand it, you're just going to *love* math."

"That will be the day." Jessica groaned.

But she paid strict attention to Randy as the two huddled over the book. He picked out a couple of problems and showed Jessica how to solve them. Then he reviewed some of the basics with her. At the end of an hour he closed the book with a bang. Grinning, he pushed it away. "See," he gloated. "Equations are just a piece of cake."

Jessica made a face. "Not for me," she said. "They just aren't any fun at all." She shook her head. "Nothing like computers," she went on, hinting broadly. "Now *they're* fascinating."

"You bet they are!" Then Randy caught on. "Want to run a program or something?"

"Oh, Randy!" Jessica trilled, pretending to be surprised at the idea. "Could I?"

Randy was hooked. "Why not?" he asked, handing her a diskette. "Let's see what you can do."

Jessica switched on the computer, inserted the diskette, and booted the machine while Randy watched over her shoulder. "You're absolutely sensational." His eyes glowed with enthusiasm. "Pretty soon you'll know as much about computers as I do."

"Oh, no," she said modestly. "There are a million things you must know that I could never even think of learning."

"Like what?" he challenged.

Jessica hesitated, swallowing hard before she said, "I read somewhere about plugging into other computers or something. Do you know what I mean?"

Randy nodded, and Jessica went on. "Into a network, I think it is."

"Oh, that! Sure. People do that," Randy replied.

"Do *you* know how?" Jessica seemed innocent as a baby as she waited for him to answer.

"Sure. It's no big deal."

"Could you show me?" Jessica asked.

"Sure! But, hey—that's illegal, you know."

"But it wouldn't hurt if you just showed me!" Jessica urged.

59

"Well . . ." Randy said, scratching his head. "I don't know."

"Please . . . for me?"

He shook his head, reluctant to do what Jessica asked, but he couldn't resist Jessica's charms. "OK," he said, sucking in his breath. "Here goes."

He plugged in a cable and pressed a couple of keys. The screen lit up, and the question "Password?" flashed across it. Then he typed out something. In no time flat the screen was loaded with information about the sales of a real-estate company in the Valley.

"It works," Jessica shrieked. "It really works!"

"Of course it does. Want me to try something else?"

Jessica's eyes glowed. "Oh, yes."

Randy typed out another command. This time he plugged into the data bank of a lumber dealer. The third time around, Randy came up with reports from a record manufacturer.

Jessica was breathless with excitement. "It's what Elizabeth called it in that story she wrote for *The Oracle*," she said. " 'The wave of the future.' " And then, as if the idea had just occurred to her, she asked, "Could you actually plug into the computer at school? The one the Morrows gave them? The one that keeps track of grades?"

"I probably could," Randy said. "But I shouldn't."

"Why not? At least then I'd know where I stand."

"I shouldn't, Jessica. I shouldn't even be doing this."

"Oh, come on," she wheedled. "It's not like I'm asking you to plug into the Pentagon or the FBI or something important."

"Not exactly," Randy agreed. "But it still isn't right."

"It isn't really *wrong*, though," Jessica argued. "Anyway, no one else will know."

Randy hesitated. Something warned him there was trouble ahead.

But as Jessica looked at him with her lower lip thrust out in the slightest, most adorable pout he'd ever seen, Randy's defenses collapsed. "All right," he said. "Here goes."

When he brought up the school records, Jessica was ecstatic. "Oh, Randy," she said, throwing her arms around him. "You must be the smartest person in the world!"

Randy's face turned such a bright red he looked like a freshly boiled lobster. "I wouldn't say that," he said, shuffling his feet. "I'm just pretty good at math, that's all."

"And a computer whiz, too." Jessica scanned the screen, and her eyes narrowed. "Could you find out what *my* grades are?"

"All of them?"

"Just the math." Jessica smiled radiantly.

"I'll try," he offered.

When she saw the F, Jessica's smile faded,

61

and her face clouded over. "Oh, no! That's what I was afraid of."

"It'll be all right," Randy said. "After what you've learned today, you'll pass the next test with no problem."

"Not me." She moaned. "I just get so scared when I take tests I can't even think straight. Even when I know the answers."

Jessica buried her face in her hands and forced tears into her eyes. "Oh, Randy, what can I do? If I don't pass, my parents will ground me for a hundred and thirty-seven years. And I can't be a cheerleader."

"It's not that bad," Randy said, patting her shoulder. "Nothing is that bad."

"It is," Jessica said with a sob. She peered at him from between her fingers. "You just can't imagine."

"I wish I could do something." Randy shook his head helplessly. "If you want, we could go over those problems again."

"That won't help. Like I said, nothing will."

"Come on. Something will turn up."

Jessica let her hands fall to her sides. Then she stared at Randy with a heartbroken expression. "Nothing will help," she wailed. "Nothing. Unless—maybe that grade could be changed. . . ."

"You mean . . . ?" Randy asked, horrified.

Jessica nodded.

"Oh, no, Jessica. I couldn't do that. I shouldn't even have plugged into the data bank.

But changing your grade? That would be a terrible thing to do."

Jessica wiped away a tear. "I wouldn't ask if I weren't so absolutely desperate."

"Gee . . ."

Now Jessica sobbed brokenly. "I don't know what I'll do."

"Don't cry, Jess." Randy put his hand on her shoulder. Then he fished a tissue from his pocket and handed it to her.

Jessica wiped her tears. "I guess I'll survive," she said miserably.

Randy stood beside her, wringing his hands. Then at last he said, "OK, I'll do it." He swallowed hard. "What do you want?"

Jessica managed a feeble smile. "A C-minus would do," she said.

Randy typed some information into the computer. "OK," he said. "All set."

Jessica's face broke into a warm, sunny smile. "You did it!" she said, throwing her arms around him. "Oh, Randy! You're just wonderful."

He gulped and turned scarlet again. "It's you who's wonderful, Jessica," he said. He scuffed his foot on the carpeting. "I was wondering, can I take you out tonight? We could go to the Dairi Burger for something to eat, then maybe to a movie."

Jessica's face fell. "I'd love to, Randy. I really would. But not tonight. Some other time, maybe. But right now I have to get home. Could you drive me back?"

Randy swallowed hard a couple of times. When he spoke his voice was so low Jessica could barely hear him. "Yes," he said. "I understand.

"Come on," he said at last. "I've got a lot of studying to do tonight anyway."

Six

Later that afternoon Elizabeth lifted a sweater from her bureau drawer, folded it neatly, and put it back. She picked up another, scrutinizing it carefully. "This one goes to the cleaner," she muttered, discovering a spot on the front of it. The spot hadn't been there when she'd worn the sweater, she thought, so it must have been Jessica's doing. Elizabeth sighed and tossed the sweater aside just as Jessica burst into the room.

"Oh, Liz! Guess what?" she said, throwing herself on the bed.

"From the look on your face, I'd say you've just been named Miss America."

"No. Guess again."

"You're getting straight A's."

"Close."

"Well?"

"I'm passing math!"

"Pinch me," Elizabeth said. "Pinch me and wake me up."

"It's true," Jessica gloated.

65

"How did that happen?"

"Maybe I'm psychic," Jessica said quickly, trying to gloss over her sister's question.

"If you're psychic, maybe you can tell me what happened to my new cashmere sweater."

"What?"

"You heard me!"

"Oh, Liz!" Jessica said. She picked up a pillow and threw it at her sister.

"OK. Bring it back. But clean."

"Sure."

Elizabeth turned her attention to her closet. When she emerged with a pair of shoes that needed heels, Jessica was standing in front of Elizabeth's full-length mirror, staring at herself glumly. "Liz," she asked, "is something wrong with me?"

"Lots of things," Elizabeth teased. "But if you've managed to pass math, I don't see why you're worried."

"It isn't that," Jessica said. "It's just that . . . well, do you think I've lost all my charm? Do I have wrinkles? Is my hair gray?" She tossed her head, and a silky web of gold flew about her shoulders. "Am I *old*?"

Elizabeth dropped what she was doing and went over to her twin. She scrutinized Jessica's face and hair. "You look about the same to me," she announced. "Of course, you *are* getting older."

"Elizabeth Wakefield! What a terrible thing to say!"

Elizabeth shrugged off the remark. "Aren't we all?" she asked.

"Yes, but there are times when I think that no one in the world cares about me."

"No one? Or one special person?"

"Nicholas Morrow," Jessica said and sighed. "Liz, do you think he's terribly cruel and callous?"

"Not from what I've seen," Elizabeth replied. Quickly she added, "He's so concerned about Regina. He was friendly enough when he was here at the party, and when we met him at the mall too."

"Then why hasn't he called me?" Jessica wailed. "I've called him half-a-dozen times to let him know I could go out with him any time he wants. But—" She spread her hands wide in a gesture of sheer despair. "It's no use."

A rush of guilt swept over Elizabeth at the misery in her sister's voice. She tried to hide it, saying, "Give him time, Jessica."

But Jessica went on complaining. "Oh, Liz! No one in the world cares about me. Not really and truly!"

The telephone rang just then, cutting short Jessica's laments. Elizabeth picked it up. "Someone does," she said, handing it to her twin. "Randy Mason."

Jessica thought she'd scream if he had called to ask for another date. But with Elizabeth beside her, she merely turned up her nose at the mention of his name. She took the phone, smothering a yawn. In a thoroughly bored voice she said, "Randy? Oh, sure. . . . Gee, Randy, it's great to hear from you. But, no. No, I couldn't possibly. I told you before. Not tonight."

She banged the receiver down so hard that Elizabeth jumped. "Hey!" she said in astonishment. "I thought you and Randy were becoming friends."

"Oh, Liz!" Jessica smothered another yawn. "Don't be a bore."

She settled herself on Elizabeth's bed, sitting cross-legged and rocking back and forth. She was such a picture of despair that Elizabeth started to feel sorry for her. But before she could say anything, the telephone rang again. Once more Elizabeth picked up. "Hi? Oh, Randy . . ."

"Jessica," he said desperately, mistaking Elizabeth for her twin. "Jessica."

"Just a sec."

But Randy was already blurting out, "Jessica, do you have any idea what I've done?"

Elizabeth tried to interrupt him, but he was either too upset to hear her or too upset to stop. "When I changed your math grade, the way you asked me to . . ."

Elizabeth sucked in her breath, then shot an angry glance in Jessica's direction. Jessica had slipped off the bed and was rapidly moving toward her own room, leaving Elizabeth to handle the situation by herself.

"Plugging into a computer that way, and then changing the data, the way I changed your grade . . . that's a federal offense, Jessica. I could go to jail. And even if I don't"—his voice broke—"if anyone finds out, I'll never get a job as a systems programmer, or anything else."

Randy's voice broke again. Elizabeth racked her brain for something to say to him. But before she could gather her thoughts, he went on. "My whole future's at stake. Do you realize that?"

Again Elizabeth searched for an answer, and again Randy rushed on, not giving her a chance to speak. "So I thought about this, Jessica," he said, "and I decided what I had to do. I'm sorry, but it just wasn't worth risking the rest of my life for something like this. So I tried to change your grade back. But I couldn't do it!" Randy's voice rose in panic. "The school's changed their computer access code. I think that someone must have realized that we were fooling around with the computer. They may be after us!"

Elizabeth gasped in concern.

"Yes!" Randy sounded as if he was on the verge of tears. "So I'm going to do the courageous thing and turn myself in," he said. "I'm going to the principal's office to tell Mr. Cooper what I've done." There was a bitterness in his voice that made Elizabeth's heart ache as he said, "Oh, it probably won't do any good, but I have to tell him."

Randy sighed and said, "That's what I'm going to do. But I had to tell you first." Then, in a voice choked with emotion, he added, "It would help a lot if you'd go with me, Jessica."

When Randy finally stopped, Elizabeth did her best to calm him, although she was furious herself. "I'll be there," she promised. "I'll definitely be there."

She heard the click as Randy hung up his telephone. Then she slammed her own down so hard she was afraid at first that she'd broken it. Then she stormed into Jessica's room.

Jessica was busily pawing through a pile of clothes in her closet, looking for the blouse she planned to wear to school the next day. She looked up as Elizabeth burst into her room. "Elizabeth," she reproached. "You didn't even knock."

"That's a laugh, coming from you," Elizabeth snapped.

"Oh, Elizabeth," Jessica said wearily. "There you go again. Grouchy as a bear."

Elizabeth ignored the remark. "That was Randy Mason," she said.

Jessica whirled around to face her. "I *know* that," she said. "Do you think I'm deaf?"

"I think you're utterly—utterly—" Elizabeth spluttered, trying to find a word to describe her feelings about her twin.

"Elizabeth, what *is* the matter with you?"

"Just that Randy told me what you did this time."

"Me?" she asked innocently. "What did *I* do?"

"You got Randy to plug into that new computer at school and to change your math grade!"

"Oh, that," Jessica said, smiling sweetly. "Randy was so nice, Elizabeth. I told him how worried I was about failing math, and he knew so much about computers, and it was all so easy for him—"

"And he could even go to jail for it."

"Oh, no. I don't think so."

"Well, he's on his way to tell Mr. Cooper what he did." Jessica's smile faded, and her eyes widened with sudden fear. "And you're going with him, Jessica."

Jessica shook her head. "I can't," she said. "I'm really awfully busy right now."

"You're going, Jessica. If I have to pick you up by the scruff of your neck and deliver you to Mr. Cooper's office myself!"

Jessica shook her head again, and now her lip quivered. "I can't, Liz," she said, pleading with her twin.

"And why not?"

"I just can't!"

"You'd be surprised at what you can do," Elizabeth said grimly.

"No, Elizabeth. Don't make me. It isn't fair."

"Lots of things in life aren't fair." Elizabeth was even more grim. "But this isn't one of them."

"Please, Liz," Jessica wailed.

71

"Get ready, Jessica. Randy's already on his way to Mr. Cooper's office."

It wasn't often that Elizabeth spoke to Jessica in such a forceful tone. But when she did, Jessica listened. She wiped away a tear and glowered at her twin. "All right," she whimpered.

"Let's get going," Elizabeth said. She went out and got the car, then drove it around to the front of the house. When Jessica didn't appear, she punched the horn with her fist. She was about to give it another blast when Jessica came flying out the door.

"You're so impatient, Elizabeth," she said, climbing in beside her. "Can't you ever learn to take things easy?"

Elizabeth bit back a spiteful response. Much as she loved her sister, there were times when she wanted to strangle her.

Starting the car, Elizabeth swung out into the traffic. She kept her mind on the road, driving fast but skillfully. It was only a few minutes before she pulled into the parking lot at the high school.

"All out," she said as Jessica cowered in her seat.

"Let me have a minute to collect my thoughts," Jessica pleaded.

"You should have done that *before* you got Randy into this mess," Elizabeth told her. "Now's the time to try to get him out of it. So come on."

Jessica dragged herself from the car. "OK," she said, slowly following Elizabeth into the school.

They headed straight for the principal's office. When Rosemary, his secretary, looked up, Elizabeth asked, "Is Mr. Cooper in?"

"He's in," she said, nodding, "but he's busy right now."

"Is he with Randy Mason by any chance?" Elizabeth asked, while Jessica hung back, scrutinizing her nails.

"How did you guess?"

"Never mind how," Elizabeth said. "Please just tell him that Jessica and I are here. He's expecting us."

"Well, if you say so." Rosemary got up and knocked on the closed door.

Mr. Cooper—"Chrome Dome" to the kids at Sweet Valley High—yelled out, "Didn't I tell you I didn't want to be disturbed?"

"Elizabeth Wakefield is here with her sister Jessica," Rosemary said quietly.

"Elizabeth and Jessica?" There was a pause, then Mr. Cooper said, "Show them in."

Rosemary nodded to the twins and opened the door. The two went into the principal's office, where Randy was sitting in a chair drawn up to the desk, his face white as a ghost's. His fingers were drumming nervously on the desktop, while Mr. Cooper stood at the window, staring out.

He spun around when the twins walked in.

Then he fixed his eyes on Jessica. "Well, Jessica," he shot at her, "what do you have to say for yourself?"

"Not a lot," she said blithely. Her smile would have melted a heart of stone.

But it had no effect on Chrome Dome. "Sit down," he growled. "And let me hear it."

"I'm sure there's some mistake—" Jessica began.

"You mean Randy didn't change your grade?" Mr. Cooper's eyebrows shot up.

"Oh, yes." Jessica smiled again. "But he didn't mean any harm." Mr. Cooper stared stonily at her, and Jessica added, "We were just fooling around."

"We? Randy says he's responsible."

Elizabeth's eyes were fixed on her twin's face. *Don't put all the blame on him*, she urged silently.

She held her breath. Then, to her relief, Jessica admitted, "I guess we both were."

"All right," Mr. Cooper said. "Let's have the whole story."

Jessica pushed her hair out of her eyes with the back of her hand. "I just asked Randy to teach me about computers." She shivered beneath Chrome Dome's icy stare, then decided to brazen it out. "It wasn't any big deal," she said.

"Didn't you plug into the school computer?"

Again Elizabeth silently pleaded with her twin. *Say "we" did it, Jessica. Please.*

Once more, Jessica seemed to hear. "We must have," she said, "if we changed my grade. But that's not a crime. Is it?" Then she gasped. Hadn't Randy told her it *was*? Her voice trailed off as Mr. Cooper's eyes bored through her. "Is it?" she whispered.

"It could be!" Mr. Cooper's tone sent chills racing up and down her spine.

He'd been pacing across the room. Now he sat down at his desk. There was a long, terrible silence. Then Mr. Cooper said, "You know, I could suspend you both for this."

Randy trembled and Jessica turned pale. "You wouldn't do that, would you?" she asked, suddenly on the verge of tears.

"I might," he said coldly.

Jessica's tears spilled over and streamed down her cheeks.

Elizabeth watched her, torn between pity for her twin and dismay at what she'd done. *How could you be so dumb, Jessica?* she thought to herself. *Couldn't you see what you were getting into?*

But angry as she was, Elizabeth couldn't bear to see Jessica so unhappy. She spoke for the first time. "Oh, Mr. Cooper," she said, tears in her own eyes now. "Please give them another chance. I know they didn't realize what they were doing!"

"That excuse doesn't wash, Liz," Mr. Cooper said coldly. "They're both old enough to know better."

"But people make mistakes!" Elizabeth

pleaded. "Jessica just didn't think this through. And I guess Randy didn't either."

Mr. Cooper scratched his chin thoughtfully. When he didn't speak, Elizabeth said, "It would be just terrible if you suspended them." Tears began to run down her face. In a choked voice she said, "Randy's whole life could be ruined. Jessica's too. Just because they made a mistake."

Mr. Cooper stared at Elizabeth while she dabbed at her tears. "And they'll never do it again," she swore. "I know they won't. They've learned their lesson, Mr. Cooper," she assured him solemnly.

Elizabeth's eyes were fastened on Mr. Cooper's face as she waited for him to speak. But he turned to look at Jessica.

"Oh, please, Mr. Cooper," Elizabeth begged. "Please give them another chance."

Mr. Cooper took a deep breath, then looked at Elizabeth again. Finally he spoke. "All right. I'll give them a chance," he said. "But only because of you, Elizabeth."

"Oh, Mr. Cooper—" she began gratefully.

He motioned to her to be quiet. "I was planning to suspend you both," Mr. Cooper said. "But Elizabeth has changed my mind."

Elizabeth sucked in her breath. Jessica wiped her eyes with the back of her hand. Randy stopped his incessant finger tapping.

"I won't suspend either of you. And I won't say a word about this to anyone, Randy, so long as such a thing never happens again."

"Oh, it never, never will," Randy swore.

Mr. Cooper held up his hand. "Hold on," he said.

"Yes, Mr. Cooper."

A hint of a smile played around Mr. Cooper's lips. "We changed our computer access code this afternoon. I'll have Jessica's grade changed back to what it was before—an F," he said. Then he stood up. "That's all now."

The three walked out slowly, each sighing with relief. Randy waved a feeble goodbye, then headed for his car. Elizabeth and Jessica followed him out to the parking lot.

Neither of the twins said a word until they were almost home. Then Jessica asked anxiously, "You won't tell anyone, will you, Liz?"

"No," Elizabeth assured her. "I won't tell."

Jessica leaned back in her seat. As Elizabeth turned into the Wakefields' street, Jessica burst out with, "Oh, Liz! I'm such a mess!"

Elizabeth reached out to stroke her sister's hand. "No, you're not," she comforted. "We all make mistakes."

"Yes, I am," Jessica insisted. "Just look at me."

Elizabeth turned to see Jessica staring into a tiny pocket mirror. "I *am* a mess," she repeated, wailing. "I've absolutely ruined my eye makeup."

Seven

As Elizabeth hurried toward the Sweet Valley High library on Friday, she spotted Regina Morrow standing alone in the hall, studying a slip of paper in her hand. Elizabeth went over to her and tapped her shoulder gently.

Regina turned quickly. "Liz!" she exclaimed, a bright smile lighting up her features.

"Need some help?" Elizabeth asked.

Regina nodded and held out the paper. "I'm trying to find this room," she said. "I'm transferring into a different chemistry section today."

Elizabeth took the slip and read the number written on it. "That's Mr. Russo's room. I'm going in that direction myself. Come on."

As they went down the hall Regina said, "I've heard a lot about Mr. Russo."

"That he's a real ogre?" Elizabeth asked, laughing.

Regina laughed, too, and nodded. "That's what I heard."

"Don't you believe it," Elizabeth said. "He's tough, but he's fair."

"So are most of the teachers here," Regina said. "I've found that out already."

"Think you'll like it here?" Elizabeth asked.

"I know I will," Regina said. "It's a lot different from back East, but so far it's been great."

"I'm glad," Elizabeth said. Then she pointed to a door just beyond them. "That's Mr. Russo's class."

Regina left her, calling out "Thanks" over her shoulder.

As Elizabeth turned away, she almost bumped into Enid Rollins. "Hey!" Enid exclaimed. "What are you doing here? You don't have class with Mr. Russo now."

"I was just showing Regina Morrow where his room is," Elizabeth said.

Normally the two would have a million things to talk about. But now they walked on in silence. Finally Enid broke it, asking, "Liz, are you still worrying about your date with Nicholas?"

Elizabeth nodded. "Is it that obvious?"

"No, not really. But I can imagine what you're going through. And from the look on your face when you mentioned Regina, I figured that Sunday night was on your mind."

"I guess it is."

"Have you told Todd yet?" Enid asked.

Elizabeth shook her head. "No, I just can't seem to tell him. I know it's silly, but I want to

79

talk to him in private, and I really haven't seen him alone since the party."

"Well, are you going out with him tomorrow?"

"Yes." Elizabeth bit her lip. "I guess it's tomorrow or never."

"Tell him, Liz," Enid urged. "Believe me, I know what can happen when you keep secrets from someone you love," she said, referring to the time she'd lost her boyfriend Ronnie because she'd kept the truth about her past hidden. "Besides," she added, "Todd's a much nicer guy than Ronnie. He'll understand."

"I hope so," Elizabeth said fervently. And at that moment she resolved to tell Todd everything on their date the following night.

From the window of her room, Elizabeth saw Todd's car rounding the corner, and she raced downstairs. Just as Todd was about to ring the bell, she opened the door, welcoming him with a "Hi!" and a ravishing smile.

"Hi, yourself!" Todd answered, catching her around the waist and pulling her toward him. He planted a long, lingering kiss on her mouth that sent chills of pure excitement racing up Elizabeth's spine.

"Expecting someone?" he said when he finally let her go.

"Sure—Matt Dillon!" Elizabeth answered, looking Todd over carefully. He was wearing a new white polo shirt that showed off his dark tan and lean, muscular build. "But I guess Matt's not coming," she joked, "so you'll have to do."

"Well, I'm looking for the most beautiful girl in the valley," Todd replied. "Is she home?"

Elizabeth poked Todd in the ribs playfully and laughed. "Seriously, Todd, you look great."

"Why not?" he asked. "Tonight I've got a date with you. Tomorrow night we're celebrating my mother's birthday. And the night after . . ."

"The game!" Elizabeth said, suddenly remembering the championship basketball game between Sweet Valley High and Big Mesa. She hadn't really forgotten it, but in the turmoil of the last few days, she'd pushed it to the back of her mind.

"The game!" Todd said, flexing his muscles. "I'm on a lucky roll, Liz, and I know we're going to win."

"Of course you are," Elizabeth responded. "But—"

"But that's Monday night. For tonight we'll make it a movie at eight, if that's OK with you."

As far as Elizabeth was concerned, anything she did with Todd was absolute bliss. "Great," Elizabeth said. "What's the movie?"

"Some horror thing. You know I'm practically addicted to them."

"I know. But I've always wondered why," Elizabeth said.

Todd's grin spread from ear to ear. "Sim-

81

ple," he explained. "You always get so scared that it gives me an excuse to hold you close."

"As if you needed one," Elizabeth scoffed affectionately. She looked at her watch. "But we'd better get going if you really want that excuse to hold me close."

"We'd better get going if I want to buy popcorn before the movie starts."

"Todd Wilkins!" Elizabeth scolded playfully. "Sometimes I think you pay more attention to your stomach than to me."

As they drove to the Valley Cinema, where the film was playing, Elizabeth rested her head on Todd's shoulder. If only this moment could last forever, she thought. If only she hadn't made that date with Nicholas. If only Sunday would never come!

Todd's voice roused her from her reverie. "*Teenage Terror*," he announced, reading the title on the marquee. "Think you can stand it?"

"Sure," she said. With Todd beside her, she could put up with anything. Not only that, but enjoy it, too.

They straggled into the theater just as the movie was about to begin. While Todd bought popcorn, Elizabeth went ahead and found seats. Then they sat together in the dark, holding each other close and munching popcorn until the lights came up again. "Like it?" Todd asked.

Elizabeth shuddered. "That was the worst yet," she said, laughing.

"I thought so, too," he agreed happily. "But

wait until next week. Meanwhile, how about some burgers? Unless all that gore spoiled your appetite."

Elizabeth giggled. "Not even the popcorn could do that," she said.

"OK," Todd said as they stepped into the parking lot. "Dairi Burger, here we come."

The street in front of the popular fast-food shop was crowded when Todd and Elizabeth reached it. "Looks like a full house tonight," Todd said, easing into a parking space. "We'll probably have to wait."

"I don't mind," Elizabeth assured him, stepping out of the car.

Inside there was a small group clustered near the entrance. But it thinned out rapidly, and in a few minutes Todd and Elizabeth found a free booth at the back. Sliding into the booth on the same side as Elizabeth, Todd draped his arm over her shoulder. They each ordered burgers and shakes.

The moment the waitress set the plate down before him, Todd picked up his hamburger and bit into it. "Hadn't realized how hungry I was," he said with a sheepish grin.

Elizabeth's head was bent over the straw stuck in her vanilla shake when she heard the front door slamming shut. Looking up she saw Betsy Martin, Tricia's sister, sauntering in with one of the disreputable boys she ran around with.

At the sound, Todd looked up, too. "Betsy

Martin!" he said. "What's she doing here? I thought she hung out at places like Kelly's," he said, referring to a seedy roadhouse that was off-limits to most of the Sweet Valley High crowd.

Elizabeth shook her head. Over the hum of voices that filled the restaurant, she heard Betsy's friend demand angrily, "What d'ya mean, no booths?"

Betsy chimed in with, "We need reservations or something? In this dump?"

"I'm sorry, but you'll have to wait your turn just like the others," the manager said, trying to calm them down. But Betsy's friend became more and more belligerent.

"Oh, Todd!" Elizabeth whispered. "I think he's drunk."

"Looks as if Betsy's had a few herself," Todd replied.

Elizabeth held her breath, waiting to see what would happen next. To her relief, Betsy and her friend stomped out, slamming the door behind them.

Elizabeth breathed more freely. "It's too bad that things are like this. Tricia's so sweet," she said, thinking sadly of her brother's girlfriend, "and Betsy—"

"Betsy's such trash!" Todd said.

"Oh, Todd!" Elizabeth's voice caught in her throat. "It's such an awful shame!"

"Hey!" Todd said, trying to lighten Elizabeth's mood. "You won't believe this, but I

84

could go for another hamburger. How about you?"

As Elizabeth shook her head, Todd crumpled his napkin and tossed it toward a coffee cup on a recently vacated table. It teetered on the cup's rim for a moment, then fell in. "Swish!" He chortled. "Score one for me."

Elizabeth giggled. "Score two," she corrected. "Oh, Todd, did anyone ever tell you you'd make a terrific basketball player?"

"Lots of people. But they ain't seen nothin' yet! Wait until Monday night, when we nail down the championship." He winked at her.

With Todd in such a great mood, Elizabeth decided the time had come to tell him about her date with Nicholas. But she'd lead up to it gradually, not just blurt it out. No one liked surprises, least of all Todd.

Fiddling with a spoon, Elizabeth said casually, "I ran into Regina Morrow at school yesterday. She's really nice."

"Yes, she is," Todd said. "But I can do without her brother."

"Nicholas is nice, too," Elizabeth protested.

"Not from where I sit," Todd answered bluntly. He sipped his shake. "But why bring him up, Liz? This has been such a great evening."

"No reason," Elizabeth said. She fiddled with her spoon again. She couldn't tell Todd about Nicholas now! So she just had to make sure he wouldn't find out somehow.

"What are you doing for your mother's birthday tomorrow, Todd?" Elizabeth asked as they got up to leave.

Todd fished in his pocket for change for a tip. "We're all going out to celebrate."

Elizabeth had hoped Todd would be more specific, but she didn't want to pry and make him suspicious. Besides, if he was spending the day with his parents, she'd be safe, wouldn't she?

Of course, Elizabeth told herself. Aloud she said, "Wish her a happy birthday for me, will you, Todd?"

"Sure will." He followed Elizabeth out of the Dairi Burger and to his car. Once inside, Todd slipped his arm around her and drew her close. Then they drove home in silence.

At her door, Todd and Elizabeth embraced again. She melted into his arms as he kissed her. "I'm going to be tied up tomorrow," he said, apologizing. "I probably won't even get a chance to call you. But you understand, don't you?"

"Sure," Elizabeth said, brushing his lips with hers in another kiss, even sweeter than the last.

She waved to Todd as he drove off, then went up to her room. *What could possibly go wrong now?* she asked herself.

Undressing for bed, Elizabeth smiled happily, remembering Todd's remark earlier in the evening. *Maybe I'm on a lucky roll, too*, she thought. Maybe everything would go just the way she hoped it would.

Maybe?

It had to!

Eight

Sunday was a beautiful day, the kind Sweet Valley was noted for. The sun was high in the sky, but the air was cool. A balmy breeze wafted a few powder-puff clouds across the horizon.

Elizabeth slipped from her bed and looked out the window. "So far, so good," she whispered to herself. But what would the rest of the day bring?

She went downstairs to a breakfast of pancakes and maple syrup. After that, she finished her homework and puttered around the house, still a little apprehensive about her dinner date.

In the late afternoon she went upstairs to shower and dress. As she stepped beneath the stinging spray, she thanked her lucky stars that Jessica was visiting her best friend, Cara Walker. With Jessica out of the way, Elizabeth wouldn't even have to make up an excuse for going out at dinner time.

Elizabeth went back to her room, patting herself dry with a huge, fluffy towel. Partially dressed, she sat down at her vanity and began to apply her makeup. A touch of eye shadow, blush on her cheeks, and lip gloss, all in soft, subtle tones. Then she dabbed some of her favorite perfume behind her ears. Her makeup on, she finished dressing.

She'd decided on a natural-silk shantung dress that was practically the color of her honey-blond hair. The style was simplicity itself, but Elizabeth dressed it up with a pair of matching shoes, a gold belt, and a bracelet. Aside from that and her watch, she wore no jewelry except for a lavaliere, one of the matched pair their parents had given the twins on their sixteenth birthday.

Elizabeth pirouetted before the full-length mirror on the back of the door. Slip showing? No, that was OK. Hemline even? That was OK, too. In fact Elizabeth could find nothing wrong with the image she saw.

Just as she was ready to slip out of the house, she heard Jessica come in. *Oh, no!* she thought, realizing that her luck had run out. Somehow she'd have to slip past Jessica. But first she'd have to hide her dress, since that would arouse Jessica's suspicions.

That seemed simple, though. Elizabeth marched to her closet, took out a light summer coat, and put it on. Then, lifting her head and thrusting out her chin, she continued her march down the stairs and toward the front door. As she neared the living room, she made her steps as light as possible.

She'd almost passed the open door when Jessica looked up from the magazine she was reading. "Hi!" she said. "Going somewhere?"

"Just over to Enid's," Elizabeth said, crossing her fingers behind her back.

"Good old Rollins," Jessica scoffed. "Honestly, Liz, I don't know what you see in her. Enid Rollins is about one hundred and thirty-seven different kinds of nerd."

"Oh, I don't think so," Elizabeth said quietly. She had no intention of getting into an argument with her twin about Enid, especially then. "I *like* Enid."

"You must," Jessica said. "Otherwise why would you be going there?"

"That's a good question," Elizabeth said as she started toward the door.

"Let me know when you have a good answer," Jessica called after her.

Once inside the Fiat, Elizabeth heaved a sigh of relief. "So far, so good," she said, repeating what she'd said first thing that morning.

She drove the car out to the street, then headed for the highway that led to Malvina, the town where the Côte d'Or was located. The roads were clear at this hour. People out for the day hadn't yet started home, and people going out for the evening hadn't yet left.

Elizabeth turned on the car radio. Jessica had set the dial to a station playing hard rock, and Elizabeth switched to one playing soft, soothing music. Then she rolled down the window and let the breeze blow through her hair.

As she drove along, she hummed to the music. By now she was sure that nothing would go wrong. She'd have dinner with Nicholas, then drive home. Jessica would never know where she'd been, and neither would Todd. And she would have kept her promise to Nicholas. What more could anyone ask?

Elizabeth turned off the highway when she reached Malvina and drove through the center of the small town, admiring the expensive boutiques on the main street and the handsome houses set back on sloping green lawns on the streets beyond it.

After a left turn, she found the narrow lane that led to the magnificent stone structure that housed the Côte d'Or. Elizabeth followed it to the gracefully curved porte cochère of the restaurant itself.

As she drove up, a liveried valet stepped forward and waved her to a stop. "Good evening," he said politely. "Shall I park your car for you?"

Elizabeth nodded, absolutely dumbfounded. After a few seconds she managed to say, "Why, yes, thank you."

The valet opened the door and helped her out. She handed him the keys, and he drove off. As she walked to the entrance she watched him.

Just then the door to the restaurant was opened, this time by a uniformed doorman.

He was just as polite as the valet, greeting Elizabeth with a pleasant, "Good evening." Elizabeth walked over to the maître d'hôtel, who was standing behind an antique desk. "Did you have a reservation, miss?"

Elizabeth shook her head. "I-I'm meeting someone here," she stammered.

"The young gentleman? Mr. Morrow?"

Elizabeth nodded. "Yes. Is he here?"

"Yes, Miss Wakefield. Right this way, please."

Elizabeth followed the maître d'hôtel through the foyer to a small room where Nicholas was waiting. When she went in, he was standing with his back to her, watching two snow-white doves fluttering about in a huge domed cage of gold. He was wearing a pair of charcoal-gray slacks and a black dinner jacket. As he turned around, Elizabeth could see the tasteful maroon ascot fastened about his neck.

Behind him, toward the rear of the room, a silver bowl filled with tiny, fresh-cut red tulips and miniature white irises sat on a lovely antique mahogany table that was placed against the wall. Near it were two small, graceful gilded chairs that looked as though they might have come from a fabulous chateau in France. On the walls were paintings that looked as though they belonged in an art museum.

"Oh, Nicholas!" she said breathlessly. "What a lovely place."

"I hoped you'd like it." He took her hand, then asked the maître d', "Is our table ready?"

"I'll check, Mr. Morrow," he said, leaving them alone.

"Have you been waiting long for me?" Elizabeth asked.

Nicholas's eyes twinkled. "All my life," he said.

Elizabeth smiled, and Nicholas checked the gold watch on his wrist. "Right on time," he assured her.

The maître d'hôtel reappeared. "Mr. Morrow? Your table is ready, sir. Will you please follow me?"

He led them to the back of a large dining room that was half-filled with guests. Just beyond, Elizabeth noticed, was the doorway to a second dining room.

"Your table, Mr. Morrow," the maître d' said. It was covered with a gleaming white damask cloth and set with glittering silver and sparkling crystal. A bowl of tiny pink rosebuds in the center was flanked by pink candles in silver candlesticks.

The maître d' lit the candles, then held Elizabeth's chair for her. When Nicholas was also seated, the maître d' handed each an enormous leather-bound menu.

Elizabeth scanned it, her eyes as bright as

93

the candle flames. "This is the loveliest restaurant I've ever seen," she said in an awed voice.

"I'm glad you like it," Nicholas said, smiling.

"Oh, I do!"

As a waiter arrived to take their order, Nicholas looked at Elizabeth over the top of his menu. "Have you decided what you'd like? Or would you rather have me order for you?"

Elizabeth closed her menu and handed it to the waiter. "I'd rather have you order," she said.

"Good. I've been planning our meal ever since you said yes." To the waiter he said, "We'll begin with the smoked salmon. After that we'll have the tournedos Rossini."

"With puffed potatoes?" the waiter asked.

"Yes. And haricots verts, too. And for dessert, we'll have the wild-strawberry soufflé."

"Very good, sir." The waiter took Nicholas's menu, then backed away, bowing slightly. A moment later a busboy appeared to pour water. Then another busboy appeared to place still-warm rolls on their plates. He was followed by still another, with tiny sculpted rosettes of butter.

Elizabeth had never felt so utterly pampered in her life. And she'd never been in a restaurant so posh, so elegant. Not even the Palomar House, the best in Sweet Valley, came close to the Côte d'Or. "Do you come here often?" she asked.

"I've just been here once," Nicholas said.

"I think I'd come here all the time if I could," Elizabeth said, as the smoked salmon was set down before her.

"No, you wouldn't. You'd be like me and prefer the Dairi Burger. Except for really special occasions, like this," he said with a smile.

Elizabeth's eyes widened. "You really like the Dairi Burger?"

"Most of the time. I have very simple tastes, Elizabeth."

"But you live in that fantastic house. Of course, I haven't seen it," she added quickly. "But Jessica told me all about it."

"If she hadn't, Cara Walker or Lila Fowler would have," Nicholas said, laughing. "They were very impressed by the house."

"Jessica said it was a mansion."

"Jessica is probably right," Nicholas told her. "But being wealthy and living in a place like that causes a lot of problems. Did she tell you that, too?"

"Jessica?" Elizabeth asked. "Never!"

"No," Nicholas said, "I guess she wouldn't." He sighed softly. Then he said, "It's wonderful to have the money to do the things you like to do. But people get strange ideas about you, too. Just because you're rich they have the notion that you're stuck up."

"Some rich people are," Elizabeth said, thinking of Bruce Patman.

"Most aren't, though. But those who are give the rest of us a bad name, so a lot of people are downright unfriendly. Then there are those who want to know us just because we have money."

"Yes," Elizabeth said, thinking of Cara Walker, "I know."

"And some—" He paused, his fork in midair. "Hey, you've hardly touched your food!"

Elizabeth looked at her plate. "You're right," she said, picking up her fork and taking a mouthful of the salmon. After she'd swallowed it she said, "This is delicious, Nicholas."

"I like it. Not quite up to the clam special at the Dairi Burger, but not so bad, either."

"Nicholas! You can't be serious. The clam special is just awful."

He laughed, then leaned across the table. "I'm serious now, though," he said quietly. "Elizabeth, I'm so glad you came here tonight."

"I am, too," she said sincerely.

There was a long silence as they finished their first course. Then the waiter appeared with a huge silver salver, topped by a silver dome. He lifted it to show Elizabeth the tournedos Rossini Nicholas had ordered.

The small steaks, garnished with crisp, puffed potatoes and slender, succulent green beans, were decoratively arranged on the tray. "It's beautiful!" Elizabeth said. "Almost too lovely to eat."

Nicholas nodded his own approval. Then he

said, "You'll change your mind when you taste it."

She took a small bite and nodded. "You're right," she said. "It's out of this world." She gazed across the table at Nicholas. "I've heard so much about you. But I don't really know anything," she said.

"Except that I'm rich!" He smiled wryly.

"That's not important," Elizabeth said. "I want to know what you're interested in. Do you like to swim?"

"Swim, yes. I play tennis, too. Do you?"

"Yes. But Jessica's the family champion."

"Maybe I'll take her on sometime. That is, if you're too busy for a game."

Elizabeth glanced at him, then went on eating.

"I ski, too," Nicholas volunteered, noticing her hesitation.

"Around here?" Elizabeth was glad he'd changed the subject.

Nicholas shook his head. "Sometimes Aspen," he said. "Sometimes Vail. And a couple of times we've all gone to St. Moritz."

Elizabeth's eyes shone. "That must have been wonderful."

"Not as nice as Zermatt in Switzerland. That's like a fairy-tale town." Nicholas paused to take another mouthful. "I always loved fairy tales when I was a kid," he said. "And I still read quite a bit."

Elizabeth nodded enthusiastically as she buttered a roll. "Who's your favorite author?"

"That's hard to say. But I've read all of Hemingway."

"He's one of my favorites, too," Elizabeth said.

"And there are a lot of mystery writers I like."

The time passed so quickly as the two discussed books that they didn't realize they'd finished the course until the busboy appeared to clear the table.

After he had removed their plates, Elizabeth asked, "What sort of plans do you have, Nicholas?"

"At the moment?" he asked, his eyes twinkling again. "Or for the future?"

"Both."

"At the moment I plan to make the most of a wonderful evening with a charming guest. As for the future, I want to go to college. I want to learn everything I can about electronics. Then I'll go into business with my father. I want to help him make the Morrow Company tops in the field."

"That's a pretty large order," Elizabeth said.

"It'll be a lot of work, but it's worth it. My father's done so much for me; I want to do what I can for him."

"That's a beautiful thought, Nicholas," Elizabeth said.

"I mean it," Nicholas answered.

Elizabeth was touched by his humility. For all his money, Nicholas Morrow was just a regular guy! She searched for something to say but was distracted by the waiter bringing dessert. The rest of the meal had been sensational, but the wild-strawberry soufflé, a puff of pink cloud, was spectacular. As Elizabeth savored the last delicious morsel Nicholas asked, "Sorry you came?"

"Not in the least," she said truthfully. "The dinner was superb. And it's been so nice being here with you."

"Care to come again?"

"No, I don't think so." Elizabeth shook her head. "As I said, it's been wonderful. But—" She paused, not wanting to hurt Nicholas.

"Yes?" he prompted.

"I'm not in love with you," Elizabeth said as gently as she could. "But I think you're one of the nicest people I've ever met."

"Thank you." A warm smile lit up Nicholas's face.

"I'm lucky to know you. I hope we can always be friends."

"You can count on me for that." Elizabeth saw the pain in Nicholas's eyes as he added, "I wish it could be more." Then he shook his head. "But you've given me the chance I asked for, Liz," he said, his smile sad.

Elizabeth sipped the coffee the waiter brought and nibbled on a petit four. *All's well that ends well*, she thought. To Nicholas she said, "It's been a really great evening."

"For me, too," Nicholas said. He reached across the table to take Elizabeth's hand.

She smiled at him over her delicate cup. Then she looked up and caught sight of someone coming toward her. *He looks just like Todd!* she thought.

Elizabeth blinked and looked again. It was Todd!

But it couldn't be. Todd was in Sweet Valley with his parents, celebrating his mother's birthday.

Wasn't he?

No, Elizabeth realized, and her heart seemed to skip a beat. Todd Wilkins was right there, in that very room. And he was fast approaching her table.

Elizabeth had a terrible feeling in the pit of her stomach. Her brain reeled. What had gone wrong?

Then it dawned on her. For Mrs. Wilkins's birthday, Todd's family had decided to splurge and come to the Côte d'Or for dinner. Now they were on their way home. And in a few seconds, Todd would be passing the table where she and Nicholas sat.

What would happen then? What would Todd say? Would he make a scene? Would there be ugly words between them?

Elizabeth couldn't bear to think about it. Her hands trembled, and a few drops of coffee spilled over and sloshed down the side of the gold-rimmed cup. She set it down with a clack. What was she to do?

She couldn't ignore Todd. And she couldn't explain what she was doing there with Nicholas. That would just humiliate the boy she loved.

In an instant an idea came to Elizabeth. She would pretend she was Jessica! It was a long shot, but one she'd have to take. In a bind like this, it was the only thing to do!

Todd drew closer, caught up in a spirited conversation with his parents. He'd almost reached Elizabeth's table when he saw her.

He stopped dead in his tracks, then did a double take. Too stunned to speak, he could only gasp, while his face turned white. Finally he croaked out her name. "Elizabeth!"

With a tremendous effort, Elizabeth pulled herself together. Then, flashing her brightest Jessica smile at the boy she loved with all her heart, she said, "You must be kidding, Todd! You mean to say you still can't tell the difference between Liz and me?" She wagged a finger at him coyly. "Wait until I tell Elizabeth. Then you'll be in trouble. About a hundred and thirty-seven different kinds."

Todd stared at her with eyes like saucers. His jaw dropped, and his mouth hung open. Todd's father guffawed while his mother tried to smother a laugh. But Nicholas, across the table from Elizabeth, was too bewildered to speak.

Todd shifted from foot to foot while a million thoughts raced through his head. *It has to be Elizabeth! It has to be!* was the first. Hot on its heels came, *But it can't possibly be. She sounds just like Jessica!*

He gave her a long, searching look as she flirted with Nicholas. Even though he could have sworn it was Elizabeth, he knew it had to be Jessica. His mind made up, he grinned. "See you around, Jess. See you, Nicholas." Then Todd walked on.

It worked, Elizabeth thought as she watched him go. Then she turned to Nicholas, who looked a little hurt and embarrassed.

Elizabeth quickly explained her odd behavior. "I've never done that before," she added. "But I just couldn't bear to hurt Todd."

Nicholas nodded. "What you did was exactly right for the moment," he said.

"Right for the moment," Elizabeth echoed ruefully. "But I should have told Todd that I was coming to dinner with you. It would have been unpleasant for us both, but I should have been honest with him. And with Jessica, too. Honesty really is the best policy."

Nicholas called for the check, paid the bill, and the two finally rose to leave the restaurant. As the door closed behind them, Elizabeth thanked her lucky stars once again. She'd courted disaster, but she'd managed to escape unharmed.

Nine

Todd stared out the window of his parents' car, peering into the darkness. He was completely wrapped up in his own thoughts. How could he have confused Elizabeth with Jessica? he wondered.

The girl in the restaurant *did* have the same sweet smile Elizabeth had. The same gentle expression. But she acted like Jessica. Besides, Elizabeth would never in the world have deceived him. He was as sure of that as he was of his own name.

Why had he suspected her? he asked himself once again.

His mother's voice interrupted his thoughts. "Todd, you're certainly quiet," she said. "Something on your mind?"

"Not really," he mumbled, still thinking of Elizabeth.

"Enjoy your meal?" his father asked.

"Yes. Sure."

"Mine was simply wonderful," Mrs.

Wilkins said. "And wasn't it a surprise, seeing Jessica there?"

"It certainly was," Todd agreed.

He felt a sharp pang of guilt for having doubted Elizabeth. He'd have to apologize, of course. And he thought it would be better to do it before Jessica broke the news to her sister.

Long before they reached home, Todd had made up his mind. He'd jump in his car and drive over to see Elizabeth. He'd tell her he was sorry, and after he'd explained, they'd have a good laugh over the whole incident.

The car slowed at last, then stopped in front of the Wilkins's house. Todd jumped out and raced to his own car, hardly waiting long enough to say goodbye.

"Todd!" his father called after him. "Where's the fire?"

"I'll be back soon!" Todd called. He hopped into his car and slammed the door. He backed it out of the driveway, then gunned the motor and took off.

A few minutes later, Todd pulled up in front of the Wakefield house. Barely taking time to set the brakes, he bounded out of the car, sprinted across the lawn to the front door, and leaned on the doorbell.

He waited, rang again, and waited once more. Just as he was about to ring a third time, one of the Wakefield twins threw the door open.

She had a white terry-cloth robe wrapped loosely around her and looked as if she'd just stepped out of the shower. Before she could open her mouth, Todd's arms were around her. "Liz!" he burst out. As the twin started to answer him, he quieted her with a long, lingering kiss.

"Wow!" Jessica whispered in a sultry tone when Todd finally released her. "No wonder Elizabeth likes you as much as she does!"

For the second time that evening, Todd did a double take. *"Omigod!"* he spluttered. "You're Jessica!"

"Very good!" She stared at him coldly. "I thought that at least you could tell us apart!"

Todd's face turned red, and he gasped like a fish out of water while Jessica waited. "Well?" There was a blast of arctic air in her voice. "What's up?"

Todd fumbled for words. "Today—today was my mother's birthday," he managed to get out. "So we all went to the Côte d'Or for dinner."

"Lucky you," Jessica said. "I wish someone would take me there."

Todd gave her a look that frazzled her hair. His voice began to rise as he lost his temper. "I ran into Elizabeth there. *She* was having dinner with Nicholas Morrow!"

Jessica blanched. "You're kidding, Todd. Elizabeth? My sister?"

"Elizabeth." Todd was in a frenzy now. Elizabeth *had* deceived him. "Your sister. And my girlfriend. At least I thought she was."

Jessica stared at Todd, her own anger mounting. Elizabeth with Nicholas? She hadn't gone to Enid's after all. Instead, Elizabeth had lied and made a play for Nicholas Morrow, the boy Jessica had claimed for her own.

Elizabeth knew how Jessica felt about him. Hadn't she confided in her? Poured out her heart? And now Elizabeth, her own twin sister, had gone behind her back and stolen Nicholas away!

Jessica was livid with rage. *Elizabeth Wakefield, just you wait*, she swore. *I'll get even with you!*

To Todd she said, "You know, you've never really understood my sister."

"You can say that again." Todd slammed his fist against the doorjamb. His voice had risen again, and now it was almost loud enough to pierce Jessica's eardrums.

Then she shouted, "Don't yell at me, Todd Wilkins!"

"I'm not yelling!" he shrieked.

"Glad to hear that," Jessica said bitterly. "But what are you going to do about this?"

Todd calmed down just enough to be coherent once more. "I'm going to tell Elizabeth that it's all over between us. Everything."

He stalked away and headed toward his car. He kicked viciously at one of the tires, then clambered into the front seat, slamming the door so hard that Jessica thought he'd shatter the car windows.

106

After Todd had driven away, tires squealing, Jessica went up to her room. She was already rehearsing what she planned to say to Elizabeth when she got home. Pacing back and forth, Jessica could hardly wait for Elizabeth to turn up. She could hardly wait for the chance to tell her twin exactly what she thought of her.

Ten

A dim light burned in the living room of the Wakefields' split-level house when Elizabeth drove up to it. Jessica's room, on the other hand, was as bright as day.

Elizabeth sighed with relief. That meant her twin was upstairs and not in the living room. And since her parents were out, she'd be able to slip in quietly without being seen. No one in the Wakefield family would ever know about this evening's escapade.

Elizabeth was glad the whole episode was over and done with. She'd had one narrow escape and was still a little shaken by it. But she'd enjoyed talking to Nicholas and was happy about the outcome of the evening.

She closed the car door quietly behind her. There was no sense in alerting Jessica now and bringing her running. Elizabeth opened the door to the house and closed it without a sound. Then she hastened upstairs to her room and switched on the light. Kicking off her shoes, she flopped down on her bed.

An instant later the door to the bathroom she shared with Jessica flew open. Elizabeth looked up to see her sister standing in the doorway, hands on her hips.

Jessica's blue-green eyes blazed with fury. Her mouth was set in a tight, grim line that, Elizabeth knew, spelled trouble. Sucking in her breath, she waited for her twin's anger to spill over. When it did, Elizabeth was surprised at the force of it.

"So how was your evening with dear little Enid?" Jessica asked sarcastically.

"Uh, Enid? It was OK. Nothing special," Elizabeth said tentatively. "We really didn't do much."

"I'll bet you didn't," Jessica said, barely controlling her fury. "But you certainly got dressed up for the occasion." She pointed to Elizabeth, still wearing her silk dress. "Just to impress Enid?"

Elizabeth's eyes widened. She tried to think of a plausible excuse. The best she could come up with was, "Enid wanted to see my new outfit."

"Too bad she didn't get a chance to," Jessica sneered.

Elizabeth sat up and swung her legs over the side of the bed. Her eyes were wide open, and her voice caught in her throat as she asked, "What are you getting at, Jess?"

"I'm getting at the fact that I don't like it one bit. Not one teensy bit. Your going off with *my* boyfriend."

"Your boyfriend?" Elizabeth was almost in shock now. "What do you mean?"

"You know what I mean. And you know who, too." She glared at Elizabeth, waiting for a response. When there wasn't one she went on. "Nicholas Morrow, that's who!" Jessica spat the name out. "Having dinner with him at the Côte d'Or!"

Elizabeth trembled slightly. "How did you know?" she whispered.

"A little birdie told me."

"Oh!" Elizabeth tried to stand, but her knees wobbled, and her legs seemed as limp as cooked spaghetti.

She dropped back down on her bed. "Did the little birdie have a name?"

"Oh, yes," Jessica said. She gave Elizabeth a withering look. "The little birdie's name is Todd Wilkins. And if you think I'm furious, you ought to see him!"

"Todd?" Elizabeth felt the same sinking sensation in her stomach that had almost overwhelmed her at the restaurant. "Oh, no!" she gasped.

"Oh, yes!"

"Did you see him? What did he tell you?"

"I saw him, all right," Jessica said. Her lips curled up in scorn. "But the point is, Elizabeth,

110

that Todd saw *you* at the restaurant with Nicholas."

"But I thought—" Elizabeth began.

"Yes?" Jessica's lips curled even more. When Elizabeth didn't answer, she went on. "I know. You thought you could go off behind my back, and behind Todd's, too, and go out with Nicholas. Well, you got caught."

Elizabeth let Jessica's words sink in, feeling worse than ever. Todd had found out, after all. But how?

Jessica lost no time in explaining. "Todd came rushing over here, all ready to apologize for mistaking you for me. And then he realized what you did to him!"

"I didn't mean to hurt him, Jessica," she said quietly.

But Jessica didn't hear. She was too caught up with thoughts of what Elizabeth had done to her. Stolen her boyfriend! Gone to dinner with him at the most expensive restaurant in the area. In a sudden rage Jessica lashed out. "How could you, Liz?" she howled. "How *could* you?"

Elizabeth's heart ached. "Oh, Jessica. I never tried to steal your boyfriend. I knew you cared about Nicholas. And I didn't want to go out with him because of Todd. I told Nicholas that."

"But you went anyway," Jessica taunted.

"Nicholas begged me to. He wanted me to get to know him. I felt I owed him that."

"You felt you owed him that," Jessica mocked bitterly. Her eyes narrowed. "But you didn't owe *me* anything! I'm your sister, Liz."

Elizabeth tried to calm her sister. "Oh, Jessica, let's not fight."

But Jessica only glared at Elizabeth. "You're jealous, Liz. That's why you made a play for Nicholas."

"I was only trying to be fair to him," Elizabeth protested. "Now that I know him, I like him as a friend. But I'm not in love with him. I'm not going out with him again."

"I suppose you told him so."

"Yes, I did. There's nothing between us, and there never will be."

Elizabeth rose from the bed and faced her twin. "I'm really sorry if I hurt you, Jessica," she said sincerely.

Jessica gave Elizabeth a sad little smile. "Well," she said, as if she were doing her sister the biggest favor in the world, "I'll forgive you this time."

"Thanks, Jessica," Elizabeth said morosely. She was glad her twin wasn't angry with her any more. But her heart ached, and her eyes were filled with tears. She'd tried to spare Todd by deceiving him and had only managed to ruin their relationship.

As Elizabeth's tears spilled over, Jessica put her arms around her sister. "There's nothing to cry about, Liz," she said. "I told you I forgive

you. And anyway, it's OK. I understand."
Elizabeth shot her twin a questioning glance.

"Well, I decided that Nicholas Morrow isn't really my type."

"Huh?" Elizabeth asked. When had Jessica given up chasing after tall, handsome, wealthy guys?

"Well, Nicholas always seems so preoccupied with his father's computer business. I mean, he rushed out of our party just so he could get to sleep early, and he couldn't spend time talking to us at the mall the other day because he had to get back to work. He never even wanted to talk on the phone. I'm surprised he found the time to go out with you!" Jessica exclaimed. "Honestly, Liz, Nicholas Morrow is as boring as Randy Mason. All those computer types are alike: dull, dull, dull!"

Elizabeth gave her sister a little smile. She suspected that the real reason Jessica had given up on Nicholas was that he had shown so little interest in her. But she didn't want to give Jessica any indication of doubt.

"Oh, Liz," Jessica began. "I'm afraid I have some more bad news."

"What now?" Elizabeth asked fearfully.

"Steve got a call from the hospital while you were away," Jessica said. "It was about Tricia Martin."

"Oh, no." Elizabeth gasped. "Is she worse?"

"Yes. She was rushed to the hospital this afternoon. She's in intensive care."

"Oh, no," Elizabeth said, shocked at Jessica's words. "Did Steve go over to the hospital?"

"I think so. He left the house after he got the phone call, but he didn't say anything."

Elizabeth waited for Jessica's usual tirade against the whole Martin family and against their brother for getting involved with one of them. But Jessica merely walked silently out of the room.

Elizabeth slipped her dress off and hung it carefully in the closet. Wrapping a robe around herself, she went into the bathroom to brush her teeth.

Distressed though she was at the news about Tricia, Elizabeth's mind was still on Todd. How on earth could she explain her date with Nicholas to him? What if she couldn't? What if Todd never spoke to her again?

Jessica's voice cut through her thoughts. "I'm about to turn in, Liz," she said in the door-way that connected her own room to the bathroom. "It's been quite a day for me."

It's been quite a day for me, too, Elizabeth thought sadly.

She said good night to Jessica, climbed into her own bed, and switched out the light. But she couldn't sleep.

Her mind was still on Todd, and after she'd tossed and turned for what seemed like forever, she picked up the phone by her bed and called him.

Todd's mother picked up at the other end. "Hello, Mrs. Wilkins," Elizabeth said politely. "Could I speak to Todd, please?"

"Todd's gone to bed."

"Could you call him? It's really pretty important."

"I'm afraid not, Liz. He asked me not to disturb him."

A chill went up Elizabeth's spine. "Oh!"

"I suppose he wants to get plenty of rest because of the basketball game tomorrow night."

"Yes," Elizabeth said. "I suppose he does. . . ." Her voice trailed off. After wishing Mrs. Wilkins a happy birthday, she said goodbye and hung up the telephone.

Now she felt worse than ever. Had Todd told his mother not to call him if Elizabeth called? Or had his mother decided that on her own? And would Todd ever forgive her?

The questions whirled around Elizabeth's brain as she tossed and turned and tossed and turned again.

It was almost morning before she fell into a troubled sleep, dreaming of Todd and Nicholas and Jessica, their faces looming large as they berated her for what she'd done. When the alarm went off, it was almost a relief.

But not for long. Elizabeth dragged herself from bed and slowly began to get ready for

115

school. Trying her best not to think of what that day would bring, she still couldn't keep her mind off Todd and what she'd done to him.

Her world had collapsed around her. Would she ever be able to set it right again?

Eleven

Elizabeth held her French book in front of her and stared at the day's lesson. She'd known it perfectly before, but now she was sure she wouldn't recognize a subjunctive if it came up and said hello.

Shifting in her seat, she glanced at Ms. Dalton. Elizabeth hoped the teacher wouldn't call on her. Not that day. Not when the only thing she could think of was Todd.

That morning in chemistry Todd had ignored her completely, and he had raced out of the class so quickly that she hadn't been able to catch up with him. Maybe she'd run into him in the hall, she thought. They *did* have history together that afternoon, but she couldn't wait that long. She had to talk to him right away. She knew that Todd had math that period. Why not be near the math room at the end of the period, when Todd would be leaving it?

Elizabeth fidgeted in her seat, glancing impatiently at the clock as she waited for the bell to ring. She headed for the door at the sound of it, then was off like a flash down the hall. When she saw Todd leaving his math class, she slowed down. It would be better not to show him how anxious she was.

Still a few yards away from him, Elizabeth waved casually and called out, "Hi, Todd."

He looked around. "Oh, hi, Liz." He walked on.

"Todd!" Elizabeth called after him.

He turned toward her. This time Elizabeth could see the hurt expression on his face. "Sorry. I've got something important to do," he said. Then he turned and walked away.

Elizabeth stood frozen to the spot, watching until he was out of sight. The bell for the next period was ringing before she could even move. Then she dragged herself slowly to class.

Somehow Elizabeth got through the rest of the day—even history class, where Todd ignored her again. Then she turned up at the office of *The Oracle*, where she was due.

Mr. Collins, the faculty adviser, looked up as she came in. Tall and slim, with strawberry-blond hair, Mr. Collins was one of the youngest and most attractive teachers at Sweet Valley High. A broad smile creased his handsome face. "Hello, Liz," he said genially. "I've been waiting for you. I've got a terrific assignment."

"Great, Mr. Collins. I need something to keep me busy."

"I figured you'd like this one," he said, his smile even broader.

"What is it?"

"I want you to cover the big game tonight."

Elizabeth's heart dropped. "Me? But what about John?" John Pfeifer was the sports editor for *The Oracle*.

"He has the flu," Mr. Collins said, "so I'm asking you to do the story."

Any other time, Elizabeth would have leaped at the chance to cover a basketball game. And to cover the championship game between Sweet Valley High and Big Mesa was something she could only have dreamed of. But now she stammered, "I-I think I'll have to pass."

Mr. Collins stared at her. "Did I hear you correctly, Liz?"

"I'm not really interested in basketball," she mumbled.

"You're not? With Todd Wilkins the star of the team?"

Elizabeth winced.

"This will be your chance to show how objective you can be, Liz," Mr. Collins said. "To show that your reporting isn't influenced by your feelings for Todd."

"I just don't think I could be that objective, Mr. Collins."

"I know you're up to it," Mr. Collins insisted.

Elizabeth shook her head. "I really don't

think I am. Besides, I've got an awful lot of studying to do."

"Elizabeth!" Mr. Collins chided gently. "You're a better reporter than that. And I know I can count on you for a terrific story."

"All right, Mr. Collins," she said finally, wondering if even a career in journalism was worth the anguish she was sure to suffer that evening.

With thoughts of the emotional ordeal ahead of her, Elizabeth hung around at home as long as she dared. When she finally reached the gym a few minutes before the game was to start, the stands were crowded.

As she looked around, she saw Enid Rollins waving to her. "I've saved a seat for you, Liz," she mouthed. It was near where Olivia Davidson was sitting with her boyfriend, Roger Barrett. Elizabeth knew she'd be safe with them.

Making her way in that direction, Elizabeth remembered how badly most of the school had treated Roger before he won Sweet Valley's Bart Race and a scholarship to Sweet Valley College. And how the gossip had spread when Jessica found out he worked as a janitor to support his family.

But things had changed fast enough after the Bart. Even Lila Fowler had made a play for him. But Roger began to go steady with Olivia, the one person who'd encouraged him in his ambition to become a doctor. And Roger had changed into a happy, self-confident guy. In the last few weeks, though, he had been moody and depressed again. When Elizabeth mentioned her concern about Roger to Olivia, she'd been shocked to learn that his father had left Mrs. Barrett and abandoned Roger.

"I was afraid you wouldn't make it," Enid said sympathetically as Elizabeth plopped down beside her. "I'm glad you did, though."

Elizabeth gave her friend a feeble smile, then slid back into the gloom that had enveloped her all day.

"Are things really that bad?" Enid asked.

"Uh-huh," Elizabeth said glumly.

"Want to talk about it?"

Elizabeth shook her head. "I don't think so. It hurts too much."

"I'm sorry," Enid said. "But if you think it would help to let it all out, I'm here."

"Thanks," Elizabeth said, glad that she had as good a friend as Enid.

Elizabeth was drawing meaningless little doodles in her reporter's notebook when the game finally started. The Big Mesa team raced onto the court first. Then Todd led Sweet Valley's squad out.

Elizabeth's heart leaped and she held her breath. She hoped Todd would give her the little sign of recognition, the thumbs-up sign, that was a ritual with them. But instead, Todd kept his eyes on the referee. Elizabeth knew it was a deliberate snub. In spite of herself, she burst into tears.

121

Through a blur, she watched as the referee tossed the ball into the air. Todd jumped for it and missed. Within seconds, the Big Mesa team scored.

They scored again when Todd's inbound throw went wide.

They scored still another time when Todd's bounce pass to Tom Hackett was blocked. And after Todd had gotten the ball again and dribbled it down the court, what seemed like a sure shot bounced off the backboard.

When Todd missed a jump shot, a groan went up from the Sweet Valley stands. The crowd groaned again when he missed a free throw. But as the game went on and Todd was forced out of bounds over and over again, the fans sat there, silent as stones.

There were cheers, however, from the Big Mesa fans as their team scored basket after basket. By the end of the first half, they were twenty-six points ahead, and their victory over Sweet Valley seemed certain.

As the kids walked down the bleachers at halftime, Elizabeth heard their comments. "What's the matter with Todd Wilkins?" "There's no way we can win now!" "Not a chance! Who would have thought we'd be playing so badly?"

Elizabeth tried to shut out the remarks by concentrating on the story she was writing. But what was there to say? That Todd seemed to be throwing away the game and that it was all her fault?

For Sweet Valley High, the championship now looked like an impossible dream. And Elizabeth's own life had turned into a nightmare.

She stayed in her seat and brooded over this latest turn of events. Then she was startled by a familiar voice.

Elizabeth looked up to see Nicholas Morrow standing beside her. "What's going on around here, Liz? Todd's supposed to be some sort of superstar, but he's hardly scored all night. And why are you so gloomy?"

Once again tears spilled down Elizabeth's cheeks. "It's all my fault," she sobbed.

Nicholas shook his head emphatically. "That just can't be, Elizabeth. It's Todd down on that court, not you."

"But if it hadn't been for me, he'd be playing the way he always does." Miserable though she was, her eyes flashed with fire. "Like a superstar," she said proudly.

"You really love him, don't you?" Nicholas asked.

Elizabeth nodded. "Yes," she said. "But Todd's never going to speak to me again."

"Of course he will," Nicholas said, trying to comfort her.

"No, he won't." And again tears welled in her eyes.

"Want to tell me why?"

Elizabeth shook her head. But before she

123

knew it she was telling Nicholas what had happened. "And the worst of it," she ended, "is that Todd counted so much on leading the team to the championship. Now I've ruined that for him, too."

Nicholas's eyes were filled with pity. He took Elizabeth's hand. "I can't tell you how sorry I am," he said sincerely. Then he straightened his shoulders and threw back his head. "But I intend to do something about it."

"It's too late," Elizabeth protested feebly.

"The least I can do is try."

"Just what do you plan to do?"

"I'm going to talk to Todd," Nicholas said. "I'm going to tell him the truth."

Nicholas strode into the locker room and looked around. Todd Wilkins was sitting alone on a bench, staring dejectedly at the floor. When Nicholas called his name, Todd looked up. Then he looked away again and mumbled, "What do you want?"

"Just to talk to you, Todd."

"Well, I don't want to talk to you."

"I don't blame you," Nicholas said. "But I'd like to explain. And to apologize, too."

Todd turned and stared at Nicholas, his eyes wide with surprise. But his doubts still nagged at him. How *could* Nicholas explain what had happened?

Todd stared at him for a moment, then

shrugged. "OK. Let's hear it. But make it quick. I'm due back on the court in a minute or two."

"All right. But first, hear this. Elizabeth would never deceive you. She'd rather die than hurt you. That's the truth."

"Yeah? Then why did she go out with you?"

"Because I practically begged her to. I put a lot of pressure on her. I know now that I shouldn't have. But I wanted to take her out so much, to see how she felt about me once she got to know me."

"Well, she knows you now," Todd muttered.

"Yes," Nicholas said sadly. "But she loves *you*."

"She told you that?"

"From the very beginning."

"But that was before she went out with you," Todd objected.

"And after she went out with me. And about two minutes ago, too."

Todd jerked his head around until he faced Nicholas. "She did?" he asked, stunned.

"She certainly did."

Todd stared at Nicholas for a long time. Had he heard right? And if he had, was it really true?

Suddenly he sprang to his feet and let out a loud, exultant whoop. "Then everything's different!" he shouted, throwing his arm over Nicholas's shoulder.

Nicholas patted Todd on the back. "Not different at all," he said. "Everything's just the way it's always been."

The Todd Wilkins who raced onto the court was far different from the one who'd meandered onto it for the first half. His step was lively, and his face glowed with happiness.

He glanced up at the stands, searching for Elizabeth. Her eyes, though, were glued to her writing pad.

If she concentrated on the story Mr. Collins asked for, she reasoned, she might not feel the terrible pain that had nagged at her during the first half. "After a disappointing beginning—" she wrote, hoping against hope for something more in the second half. She paused, then bit the eraser on her pencil.

Just then the game started, and a roar went up from the Sweet Valley stands. When Elizabeth looked up, she saw Todd dribbling the ball so fast that everything seemed blurred.

Then *swish*. He dropped the ball effortlessly into the basket. "Way to go, Todd!" someone shouted. "Way to go!"

From that point on, Todd was in complete control. He scored again and again.

For a minute Elizabeth stared open-mouthed. Then she bent down to finish her sentence. "After a disappointing beginning, Todd Wilkins showed the stuff heroes are made of."

Two more points for Sweet Valley. *Come on, Todd. I know you can do it*, she whispered to herself.

And it was almost as if he heard her. He was off again and running. And scoring, too.

But great as Todd was, he was competing with a team that was almost as good. It just didn't seem as though there was any chance of overtaking the lead Big Mesa had racked up in the first half.

Still, the figures on the scoreboard kept climbing. By the end of the third quarter, Big Mesa's lead had been cut in half.

The final quarter started with the fans on both sides going completely crazy. Down on the floor it was bedlam as the two teams battled it out for the championship. On the scoreboard the figures for Sweet Valley High crept up nearer and nearer to those for Big Mesa.

There was another mighty roar from the Sweet Valley stands that seemed to shake the rafters, as Todd sent still another shot through the hoop. Elizabeth, scribbling frantically, looked at the scoreboard and saw that Sweet Valley now lagged by only five points.

Then three.

Then one!

But that one point was crucial. And try as they might, it seemed that Sweet Valley would never catch up.

"The game turned into a real cliffhanger," Elizabeth scrawled in her notebook. "With less than a minute left to the game and only one point between the two teams—"

There was another roar that shook the building. When Elizabeth looked up again, Todd was poised to shoot.

With the grace and skill of a superb athlete, he sent the ball spinning off toward the hoop. It hovered on the rim, revolving lazily. A hush fell over the crowd as everyone waited to see if it would drop in.

Elizabeth held her breath and looked at the scoreboard clock. Three seconds left.

Swish!

It was in! As the buzzer sounded, the Sweet Valley fans went wild. The game was over, and their team had won!

The screams from the fans around her nearly shattered Elizabeth's eardrums. An instant later most of the kids were swarming onto the court, still screaming. Jim Daly and Tom Hackett hoisted Todd to their shoulders, then carried him around the court. The cheerleaders, with Jessica spurring them on, shrieked and howled and whistled, while Todd beamed and waved.

As Todd was carried off, Jessica climbed up into the stands, looking for her twin. "Wasn't Todd something?" she asked. "I knew we'd win. Didn't you?"

"Oh, sure," Elizabeth said despondently.

"And we did," Jessica gloated. "And, Liz, there's going to be the most fabulous party at Cara's place. Absolutely everyone's going to be there."

"I don't think I'll go," Elizabeth informed her twin.

"You have to. How else will I get there? Or get home afterward?" Jessica's eyes narrowed.

"Couldn't you ask someone to take you?" Elizabeth answered.

"Oh, Liz! It would be so humiliating for me to ask for a ride to a party," Jessica wailed.

"If only you had the car," Elizabeth interrupted. She was too tired to argue about it now.

"If I had the car, I could drop you off somewhere and then go on to the party."

"Thanks. But I'll walk."

"Have it your way. But really, Liz. I don't think you should be driving. And you can explain to Mom and Dad that you weren't feeling well and asked me to give you a lift," Jessica schemed.

"Take the keys." Elizabeth sighed and tossed the keys over. "I'll explain."

"Oh, Liz," Jessica shrieked before dashing.

Blinking back her tears, Elizabeth watched her sister go. Todd had won the game and the championship he'd set his heart on. But she had lost everything.

Twelve

Elizabeth waited in the stands until the gym was almost empty. Then she crept down the stairs and went outside.

It was so late that the lights in the parking lot were being turned off. But that was fine with her. That way she wouldn't run into any of the kids from Sweet Valley.

Outside the school, she stopped. She had a long way to go. A line from a poem she'd studied in English came back to her: "And miles to go before I sleep." It was by the poet Robert Frost, and Elizabeth had been so moved when she first read it that she had almost cried. It was then that she'd vowed to do her very best, no matter what she wrote.

As she started home with those lines whirring through her mind, she repeated that vow to herself. No matter what had happened between her and Todd, and no matter how close she was to tears, she'd at least turn in the best story to Mr. Collins she possibly could. She owed that to him, and to herself, too.

Elizabeth had already thought of an opening line and was blocking out the rest of the story as she walked along.

Suddenly, though, she heard footsteps behind her. Elizabeth didn't know whether to stop or to run away.

She was still trying to make up her mind when she felt a hand on her shoulder. Then she felt herself being spun around as if she were a top. Todd Wilkins stood before her, and she couldn't think of a thing to say except "Oh!"

But that was all right because she couldn't have gotten a word out anyway. Todd pressed his lips against hers and gave her a kiss so long and so deep and so sweet that Elizabeth knew there was no mistake about it. Todd had forgiven her.

It was a long time before Todd released her. Then, when he at last stepped back, the two stood silently in the moonlight, in the shadow of a magnificent acacia tree.

Elizabeth still couldn't think of anything to say except, "Oh, Todd!"

Still, it wasn't long before her words came rushing out. "Todd," she began, "I don't know how I can explain to you what happened."

"You don't have to, Elizabeth." He grinned sheepishly. "Nicholas Morrow did. You know, he's not such a bad guy after all."

131

"He's pretty nice. Not like you, of course, but he's pretty nice."

"He told me how he put all that pressure on you to go out with him," Todd said. "And how you didn't want to. You must have practically flipped when I ran into you at the Côte d'Or. Imagine that! At the Côte d'Or. The only time in my life I've ever been there!"

"The only time I have, too," Elizabeth chimed in.

Todd stared off into space. "Can you imagine what the odds are on something like that happening? A million to one, I'd bet. Or five million." He shrugged his shoulders. "Or maybe even a billion. Who knows? You'd probably have to work it out on a computer."

"No, thanks," Elizabeth said, laughing. "I think I'll pass on that one."

"Now what does that mean?" Todd asked, puzzled.

But Elizabeth had no intention of telling him about the awful mess Jessica had gotten herself and Randy Mason into—not after she'd promised her twin never to mention it to anyone. *A promise is a promise*, she reminded herself. Although, she had to admit ruefully, sometimes keeping a promise could cause a lot of trouble. Under those circumstances, she made herself a promise—never to make promises again.

The idea appealed to her so much that she giggled. Once again Todd was puzzled. "What's so funny?"

"I don't know," Elizabeth said, still giggling. "It's just that life gets so complicated at times. Still, things always seem to work out in the end."

"That's a very profound thought, Elizabeth Wakefield," Todd said with a wink. "But this is hardly the time for profound thinking, is it? Not with that full moon overhead and the soft breeze blowing."

"And the two of us just standing here?"

"Just standing here wasting our time, when there are things so much more important we could be doing."

"Like what?" Elizabeth asked.

"Like this." Todd slipped his arm around her and drew her close. Their lips met again in a long, passionate kiss. As if to give them a bit of privacy, the moon slipped behind a huge, fluffy cloud. It didn't reappear until the two broke apart once more.

Then Todd looked at his watch. "Oh, my gosh," he said. "Do you know what time it is?"

"I don't really care," Elizabeth whispered, ruffling his hair. "I could just stay here like this all night. But I know that everyone must be waiting for you. After all, you're the hero of the evening."

"Hero's a pretty fancy word. I really didn't do so much."

"You only won the championship for Sweet Valley High." She kissed him lightly on the forehead, then sighed. "But you're right. We'd better get to that party. And we'd better get going. It's a long walk to Cara's place."

"It's a much shorter walk back to the parking lot," Todd said, taking Elizabeth's hand.

It *was* shorter, Elizabeth thought, as they neared Todd's car. Far too short, in fact. And it had seemed so long to her when she'd been walking away.

The lights were bright at the Walker home when they drove up. Through an open window they could hear the sound of music, played by The Droids.

It stopped, though, when they went inside. A rousing cheer went up for Todd. He beamed and, holding Elizabeth's hand in his, lifted them both high in the air. At that moment, The Droids broke into one of Sweet Valley High's fight songs.

Todd and Elizabeth wandered through the room arm in arm, greeting everyone while Todd gracefully accepted their compliments. "Todd, the game was terrific!" Jessica said excitedly.

Cara Walker was equally effusive. "The greatest ever!" she gushed.

Then Nicholas Morrow came up to the pair. He clapped Todd on the back and said, "That was one of the most exciting games I've ever seen, Todd. You were really sensational."

Todd smiled his thanks. "Well, I owe a lot of it to you," he said.

"To me?" Nicholas asked.

"Don't be modest, Nicholas. You know that

if you and I hadn't had our little halftime conference, Big Mesa would have won the championship. And I would have lost Elizabeth," Todd added quietly.

"Let's forget about it, OK?" Nicholas suggested.

Todd nodded.

"But before it's all forgotten," Nicholas said, "do you mind if I dance just this once with Elizabeth?"

Todd grinned. "She's all yours," he said. "For about five minutes," he added, grinning even wider.

As Nicholas walked Elizabeth to the dance floor he asked, "So is everything settled between you and Todd now?"

"Oh, Nicholas," Elizabeth said enthusiastically, "it couldn't be better. Thank you so much for straightening things out."

"Well, it was the least I could have done. After all," he said with a broad grin, "what are friends for?"

Elizabeth gave Nicholas a warm smile. "We will be friends," she said sincerely. "Forever."

"Then let's dance—to our friendship," Nicholas said as he put his arms around Elizabeth.

They had just begun dancing when Elizabeth felt a tap on her shoulder. She turned to see Cara Walker. Elizabeth gave her a puzzled look.

"Your mother just called," Cara said to

Elizabeth. "She wants you to call her back right away."

"My mother? I wonder why she would call me here."

"I don't know, but she sounded sort of worried. Why don't you call from my father's study?" Cara suggested. "It's more private. And you won't have to compete with all this noise."

Elizabeth turned to Nicholas. "Will you excuse me?"

"Of course, Elizabeth."

Elizabeth looked around. "Where's Jessica?" she asked Cara. "Maybe she should be with me."

"I'll go find her," Cara said.

Elizabeth went into the study and closed the door. Just as she finished dialing, Jessica appeared, looking frightened. "What do you think they want?" she asked. "Do you think it has anything to do with my driving the car?"

Elizabeth shook her head. "They wouldn't call us here just about that," she said.

She heard the phone ring at the other end. It was picked up almost at once, and her mother said, "Elizabeth? Is that you?"

"Yes. What's happened?"

There was a short pause, but to Elizabeth it seemed to last forever. Then her mother said, "It's Tricia Martin, Liz. It looks . . ." Her voice broke. "It looks as if the end is near."

"Oh, no," Elizabeth gasped. To Jessica, at her side, she said, "It's Tricia. She's . . ." Her voice broke, and tears began to stream down her face.

"Oh, Liz!" There was no need for Elizabeth to say more.

Elizabeth spoke to her mother briefly. Then she hung up the phone. "Maybe it's just a false alarm," Jessica said, putting her arms around her sister.

Elizabeth grasped at this slender straw. "Maybe," she said. "But Mom and Dad want us to meet them at the hospital right away. Steve's already there."

Is this really the end for Tricia Martin? Find out in Sweet Valley High #15, PROMISES.